Shift OUT OF LUCK

BRIMSTONE  INC.

Shift OUT OF LUCK

BRIMSTONE ✪ INC.

ABIGAIL OWEN

Entangled Publishing, LLC
10940 S Parker Rd
Suite 327
Parker, CO 80134
rights@entangledpublishing.com

Amara is an imprint of Entangled Publishing, LLC.

Edited by Heather Howland
Cover design by Bree Archer
Cover photography by HayDmitriy/Depositphotos
DenisTangneyJr/GettyImages
wacomka/GettyImages

Manufactured in the United States of America

First Edition April 2020

To Kaitlyn.

1

Prologue

The small chapel in the heart of the Colorado Rocky Mountains was beautifully natural, with pews carved from matching pinewood standing in rows, a single aisle down the center, and floor-to-ceiling windows at the front. The view of the lake and mountains outside glittered under the brilliant light of the full moon.

Marrok Banes didn't see any of it.

He was too busy waiting for his mate to walk down the aisle.

His *arranged* mate.

And his sworn enemy.

Marrok itched to roll his shoulders but didn't. A twitchy alpha was a dead alpha, and all eyes were on him. If Shakespeare had solved the Montague and Capulet feud by uniting the two families through a marriage of convenience, would it have looked like this?

Two alphas, mating to unite their packs. Bringing an end to their millennia-long feud.

If this worked, he'd thank Delilah later. The enigmatic

owner and operator of Brimstone, Inc., a firm specializing in all kinds of supernatural solutions—including matchmaking, it seemed—had been the one to broach the idea to him. For his pack, he'd been willing to make the personal sacrifice of mating not only a woman he didn't know, but the alpha of the pack his own people despised.

If this worked. *If* it ended the feud.

Inside, the room was packed with people, the earthy scent of so many wolf shifters in one room filling the space with undertones of moss, dirt, and stone. The majority of those here hailed from the Canis and Banes packs, a line practically drawn down the center of the chapel, with neither side willing to mix with the other.

A few snarling faces among those gathered, along with several missing elders from both packs, told him loud and clear that simply completing the ceremony wouldn't be enough. He was going to have to show this newly combined pack how to change centuries of behavior and ignore their history of mutual hatred and violence.

But they'd made plans to help with that tonight. Supernaturals were many things, and superstitious fell just below suspicious on the list, and somewhere ahead of fucking resistant to change. He wasn't above using that as leverage. No way would their packs simply ignore the wishes of the gods, which was why he and Tala had elicited the help of the nymph to fake the gods' blessing. As long as everyone in attendance believed the elaborate natural display she was supposed to conjure up to be a sign, maybe those still protesting this arrangement would shut the hell up and give both him and his new mate, and this new peace, the chance it deserved.

If not…

The organ music rose in a swell of sound, and Marrok stood taller, shoulders back, every inch the alpha his people expected him to be. The double doors to the church opened to admit Tala Canis—his new mate.

Time to create a new history.

The gathering hushed, and Marrok's entire being stilled as the visual impact of his bride in her wedding gown stole the breath from his lungs as effectively as a sucker punch to the windpipe. Damn, she was gorgeous, radiant in a formfitting dress that hugged her lithe body to her knees, where it flared out. She'd left her shoulder-length dark-blond hair down, her veil framing her lovely face.

Every man in the place had to reel his tongue back in.

No one could deny Tala—tall and slender with curves he itched to mold with his hands—was the stuff fantasies were made of. The actual mating part would not be a hardship with her.

His wolf stood to attention, rumbling happily inside his head even as he wanted to snarl at every male in the room watching her with lust. The animal part of him had a thing for his soon-to-be mate, which should make things easier, since the animal inside him usually didn't like anyone.

Mine.

The mating pheromones they were both releasing surged to life. It happened with all wolf shifter matings, and even stronger for alphas, but this was unlike anything he'd ever experienced.

He took her hand, and the strangest sensation, like a settling, overcame him at her soft touch. This was how the earth felt when the winds stilled and the sun shone down. On the back of the settling came a kick of need so violent, his dick pressed against the zipper of his pants, thick and throbbing.

He wasn't entirely sure if that were the pheromones or his sincere reaction to her.

Thankfully, the ceremony wrapped up in short order. The wedding portion of wolf shifter matings tended to be brief, as, thanks to those pheromones, everyone was itching to get to the actual mating ceremony.

He'd played it cool up until now. Though he doubted others noticed, Tala was definitely skittish, and he hadn't wanted to scare her off. But tonight…

Time to claim his mate.

Yearning and anticipation hung heavy in the air as he led his bride down the aisle, the gathering following behind in a building silence. Together they made their way out of the chapel. Their paths lit by the cool glow of moonlight, they walked along the river and over a wooden bridge that led them into the woods beyond, the peaks towering above, black outlines in a midnight sky.

Once deep in the woods, the wedding guests stopped, allowing Marrok and Tala to continue on into the trees alone. Marrok had prepared a place for them to mate in private. Despite the offer of help from many women in the pack, he'd insisted on creating this haven on his own. An odd urge to make this moment entirely between Tala and him, with no other eyes or opinions, had driven that decision. Too late now if she didn't like what he'd done.

"Stop here," he said.

She glanced his way, an alpha's instinctual need to balk at an order in her gaze, but did as he asked.

"Close your eyes."

Now she frowned, and a smile tugged at his lips. He knew what he was asking. They were both fighters, predators. Instinct screamed to watch another predator closely. He was asking for her trust.

She gave him a long, hard stare, then slowly closed her eyes.

Victory surged through Marrok, pumping even more desire into his veins like shots of adrenaline. He allowed himself a brief moment to study his mate. Flawless skin, high cheekbones, feline-slanted eyes of startling green currently hidden from him. Gorgeous.

"Are you going to stand there staring?" Tala kept her eyes closed but cocked a single eyebrow in question.

Marrok chuckled. "Just admiring what's now mine."

Something flickered across her expression, but with her eyes closed, he didn't catch the emotion. Marrok pulled one of her hands through his arm. "Keep your eyes closed."

Taking care so that she wouldn't stumble, he parted a curtain of vines that appeared to cover solid rock, but, once drawn back, revealed a tunnel large enough to stand in. He led her inside, where the air caressed their skin, cool and damp. Their footsteps, particularly with her sky-high heels—what kind of woman wore stilettos in the woods?—echoed off the stone floor, the noise pinging around them.

Tala's nose twitched. "Are we in a cave? It smells like wet rock."

"Maybe. Not much farther." Unable to not touch her any longer, he circled his thumb over the pulse point on her wrist. Her small gasp fed his growing satisfaction.

As they moved down the tunnel, a rushing sound of water grew louder and louder. Finally, he led them into a small chamber behind a waterfall. A light mist swirled around the room, which he'd lit with thousands of twinkle lights. Wanting to provide a luxurious and comfortable setting, he had brought in cushions—silk, satin, chenille, any soft materials, all in the same emerald green as his new mate's eyes—and strewn them about the cave.

"Open your eyes."

Unaccustomed nerves gripped him as she slowly lifted her eyelids and took in the scene he'd prepared for them.

No reaction.

Slowly she moved forward, taking in the details. He crossed his arms and waited. First, she examined the waterfall, trailing her hand through the downpour. With her back to him, he couldn't gauge her reaction, though. Then she crossed to the pillows and leaned over to touch one, running her long, tapered fingers over the opulent material.

His own skin tightened as though she'd physically touched him.

Finally, she swung around to face him, her expression unreadable. "You did all this for me?"

"Yes."

Confusion flashed across her features so quickly he almost didn't catch it. "But this is an arranged mating."

"It may be starting that way, but you are my mate."

She glanced away, once again taking in her surroundings. Then crossed the cavern to where he stood. With a featherlight touch, she laid her palms against his chest and gazed up into his eyes. Her one simple touch, combined with her wildflower scent swirling around him, fired his blood, but he managed to hold himself still. Waiting for her.

Slowly she trailed her hands up, under his tuxedo jacket, pushing it off his shoulders, then down over the fine linen of his shirt where she paused and undid his pants. Already hard as the granite mountains, he ached at her actions, throbbing, but held back, letting her lead for now.

Pants loose, she pulled his shirt out and started on the buttons. With each exposed patch of skin, she laid those delectable lips against him in sweet kisses which had his blood driving through his body. Marrok fisted his hands, because the second he touched her, he knew gentle and slow would be over.

At the warm flick of her tongue against the ridges of his abs, he groaned. "Tala. I can't—"

He choked off the words as she snaked a hand into his pants and wrapped a fist around his cock. She gave one hard pump and he shuddered.

Claim. His wolf paced inside his head.

He reached for her but found himself holding nothing because she dropped to her knees, freeing him from his pants at the same time.

He didn't want her feeling as though she had to. This was about both of them. "Tala—"

"I want this," she whispered.

Before he could stop her, she wrapped those amazing lips around him. Marrok's head dropped back and a feral growl ripped from his throat as his wolf howled his delight.

Marrok buried his hands in her hair, holding and guiding at the same time, and slowly pumped his hips, dragging at her plump lips, surrounded by heat and her slick, searching tongue. Once. Twice.

Sweet agony.

But his body was too primed, and she was going to send him over the edge before they consummated their mating.

"Tala," he choked.

She chuckled, the tickle of it against him making the ache worsen, but she released him and glanced up. Her green eyes now glowed. She, too, was on the edge of shifting, losing control.

Time to take over. He reached down to drag her up, but before he got a grip on her, she rolled backward and up to her feet in a move both lithe and athletic, and damn difficult in a wedding gown, he'd bet. Standing apart, gaze never leaving his, she reached for the zipper at the back of her dress. In a flash, she peeled the silken gown off her body.

Naked.

His mate had been entirely, gloriously naked under her dress this entire time? If he'd known that when she walked down the aisle, he might've mated her then and there. Screw the wait and the wedding ceremony and the audience.

"You want me, alpha?" The husky purr in her voice

flayed him. "Then come and claim me."

Her playfulness combined with challenge was like a spark to gasoline. He put on a burst of speed and had her on her back among the cushions, his body wedged between her legs, before she could even take a step.

A surprised laugh burst from her. "Hey. Big men aren't supposed to move that fast."

Wow. That smile. His heart contracted. Good thing she hadn't used that on him while negotiating this mating. "With the right motivation…"

His wolf was demanding he take her, right there, but Marrok wanted to savor his mate's body first. He dipped his head and took one tight, pink nipple in his mouth, flicking it with his tongue. With his other hand, he molded her other breast. For such a slim woman, she was a perfect handful. She squirmed beneath him and grew slicker where he lay cradled between her legs.

A rushing noise, like ocean waves coming into shore, filled the cavern. In a daze, Marrok watched the backside of the waterfall that had been showering them in mist jut outward from the cave where they hid, as though the flow was being redirected around an invisible obstacle.

Their fake sign from the gods had begun.

And right this second, he didn't give a damn. He took Tala's lips in a deep, drugging kiss, his tongue dancing with hers—unabashedly possessive, dominant, but then so was her response. The sweet, ripe-berry taste of her flooded his mouth as she answered every kiss with a needy moan.

His wolf lunged inside him, determined to take control and claim his mate. With a jerk, Marrok pulled back. "I have to take you. Now."

She gave a vigorous nod, her eyes feverish, a deep flush slashing across her cheekbones. "Do it."

"Don't let your wolf maul me." It had happened to other

couples.

In response, Tala parted her legs wider, giving him more access. With a single stroke he entered her. Marrok gave a shout of triumph as her wet heat clamped around him. Pure heaven. His muscles shook with his attempt at control. With each thrust, he dragged his cock over her sensitive nerves, each time faster, harder, and her cries and frantic hands on his body dragged him into an abyss of sensation.

More so, the way her gaze caught and held his, sharing this moment in an unexpected way.

Vaguely, all his focus on the woman driving him higher and higher, Marrok was aware of the forest outside their cave. The waterfall peeled back from the rocks. The wind whipped the trees into a frenzy. Pine needles rained down, filling the air with their zesty scent. Birds screeched their protest as they abandoned their nests and perches. The chaotic world around them echoed the desire slamming through him.

Slamming through *both* of them, if Tala's feverish, frantic movements were any indication.

He smoothed a hand over her thigh and bent her leg to wrap around him, seating him deeper inside her. Her shivery intake of breath and the way she dug her nails into his back, no doubt drawing blood, told him she liked it. Their mating might be arranged, but her body's reactions to his weren't an act, and he relished every fucking second.

Every movement, every moan, only drove him higher. Tingling gathered in his balls, pressure building. As the culmination of their mating neared, he brushed her hair back from the nape of her neck and licked at the spot he exposed.

"Ready?" he asked.

That emerald gaze had yet to leave his. "Yes."

Damn, he loved that word on her lips.

Marrok allowed his wolf to show, forcing his canines to drop, and she licked her lips, pink tongue flashing over the plump flesh. With a growl, he leaned forward and, hips pumping, cock sheathed inside her, he bit hard—sank his teeth into the sweet spot where her neck and shoulder met. The rich taste of her blood burst on his tongue.

Still he held off on reaching for his own completion until the ripple of her orgasm fluttered around his dick. That's all it took.

His body imploded, along with stars and swirls of color behind closed eyes as he continued to suck, marking her as his. His loud growl, deafening in his ears, joined Tala's scream as he pumped into his mate. Pleasure surged through him as the perfection of her body and an odd sense of connection provided an intimacy he'd never experienced before.

The cacophony of noise from the waterfall and forest beyond suddenly ceased. The water splashed back down with an almighty roar, covering them in a chilly sheen of moisture.

He continued to move inside her until they'd both wrung every ounce of pleasure from their mating. With a satisfied grin, he kissed the mark on her neck, which was already starting to heal, then pushed her sweat-slicked hair from her face.

She gazed back with wide, almost wary eyes. "Violent delights," she whispered, more to herself than him.

She was quoting *Romeo and Juliet*. Was that how she saw them? Star-crossed? Fated to end in death and defeat?

Marrok shook his head. "It's up to us to hold the violent ends at bay."

Her lips crooked, amusement swirling with determination in her eyes. "Yes, it is, mate."

Mate, his wolf crooned, equally satisfied.

This was going to work.

Chapter One

Tala hurled a knife at the target twenty feet away and pictured her mate's head.

Her *mate*.

It had been a month. Thirty-ish days of the most amazing, hot-as-sin, give-and-take nights followed by the most hair-rending, teeth-gnashing, beyond frustrating days.

Ironic, those nights, given how her own pack had written her off as a frigid ice queen before. She'd been too focused on becoming alpha to give men much thought until now. Every pack handled the selection of alpha differently. In her pack, all contenders fought until only one remained standing. She understood Marrok's pack based theirs more on bloodlines, as did many others. Hers found that led to bias, murder of siblings in the ruling family, and lack of adaptation to the ever-changing world around them.

Another knife flew, only this one missed wide, embedding in a nearby tree, sinking deep with the force of the emotions behind the throw.

Damn. She never missed like that.

Was the problem the emotions or her clothes?

She'd come from another meeting that hadn't ended well for her. As usual, for meetings, she'd dressed professionally. A sleeveless top with a square neckline and pencil skirt, she'd paired the outfit with killer black stilettos. Always present the image you want to be known by. She made sure her clothes screamed class, control, and power. Plus, the heels on her stilettos doubled as weapons in a pinch.

Marrok did the same, dressing for meetings in power suits meant to drive home his position in the pack. But the second they were alone, the jacket and tie came off and sleeves were rolled up, as though he didn't enjoy the confinement.

She kicked off her heels, set, and threw again, this knife going exactly where she wanted.

Tala gave a grim smile. At least she could control something in her life. Part of the reason she was alpha was that no one saw her coming, even when they thought they did. Secrecy and innovation were key to her brand of fighting.

She'd *earned* alpha, but, as a woman, she found she had to earn it over and over again. Every damn day.

Another knife struck true.

I have to make this mating work. But how?

Given the way things were going so far, only one month into her arranged mating, peace for the Canis pack was apparently coming at the cost of losing all the respect she'd fought for.

The faked sign from the gods had helped, but it hadn't fixed everything. If Marrok disagreed with her one more time in public, no matter how small or even reasonable, she was going to have to do something about it.

Like unleash her wolf on the man.

Not surprisingly, her inner animal gave a small growl of approval at the thought. When she'd gotten her first whiff of the Alpha of the Banes pack—mountains and rum—Tala's wolf had been practically begging for a good fucking. Hell, the hussy would've gladly rolled over and exposed her belly to him. But after the night of their mating she'd done a one-eighty, turning downright surly when it came to Marrok. Tala still hadn't figured out why. Personally, if she were less self-controlled, Tala could get drunk on his scent alone.

Granted, her mate had yet to catch on to how his taking charge in every single thing, no matter how many times she pointed out the issue in private, and it was causing her big problems. But he also treated her as though she was important to him, both publicly and privately. And the things he did to her body…

She hurled another knife, which hit the target with a satisfying thud, her aim true.

Maybe this had been his plan all along? Combine the packs and take over the weak female alpha. Though she couldn't see Marrok doing that.

Her pack members, however, didn't trust him as readily. After the last meeting, Sandalio, the most ancient member of her pack, had pulled her roughly to the side.

"You are making the Canis Pack look like fools," he'd hissed at her, his canines elongating. "Your new mate is making every decision without you. As our alpha, you should be showing the Canis dominance."

She damn well wasn't about to get into yet another debate about the combining of the packs meaning they were no longer on opposite sides. However, the need to display dominance ran strong in male wolf shifters. No wonder her kind couldn't figure out how to live in peace.

She'd yanked her arm out of his tight grasp, drew to her full height, and faced him down. "Do not assume I don't have a plan, Sandalio. And I suggest you draw in your teeth before I take that as a challenge."

The last was a command, something she tried not to use

often. She refused to be a dictator. However, sometimes she found the males in her pack needed reminding about who was boss.

Sandalio had glared but slowly retracted the razor-sharp teeth, resuming his human appearance. "We're watching." His warning had hung in the air as he'd slunk away, metaphorical tail tucked between his legs.

Asshole.

He'd never had the guts to challenge for alpha himself, but sure loved to throw his weight around. As an elder he should support his alpha and give her advice. Not threats.

A knife whistled past her ear to thud into the target she'd been using, and Tala stiffened before slowly turning to find Marrok standing behind her, an amused smile tugging at the corners of his mouth.

She had to admit, she'd lucked out in the mate department. The man was a walking cliché, with his blue eyes and dark hair. Only the gray at the temples saved him from being too pretty. That and a slightly crooked smile.

But for her it wasn't his pretty face that snagged her attention, it was his physique. At six foot four, with his broad shoulders and muscled form, Marrok was an intimidating specimen. One who knew how to use his body—in combat, in the bedroom. Hell, the way he walked was pure power.

A small part of her, goaded by her wolf, wanted to rattle his cage. Dangerous, messing with an alpha male, but she was more than capable of dealing with him.

She turned and set her feet shoulder-width apart, then raised one arm, pointing straight out, lining up the tips of her fingers with the target. Tala raised her other arm, bent at the elbow, with her hand behind her head, ready to throw.

"You forgot your knife," Marrok pointed out as he walked around to watch her from the side.

She couldn't have set it up better. With a flick of her hand,

Tala produced a knife, seemingly from thin air, and hurled it.

Rather than react with shock, Marrok crossed his arms, his gaze zeroing in on her with what she might have described as deadly intent if she wasn't his mate. And, just like that, he was every inch the alpha.

And damn it all if she didn't find him even hotter.

Her wolf, however, growled inside her. She didn't appreciate the subtle display of power one bit.

Tala ignored her animal. Rather than be intimidated, she drew on the subtle challenge, her competitive side coming to the fore. Time to show him why he should *never* underestimate her.

Another flick of her wrist, another knife appeared in her hand, which she threw with unerring accuracy. He narrowed his eyes and she delivered the sweetest smile, right before she flicked her wrist and drew forth another knife.

Her pack had learned—several of them the hard way— that Tala was never without a weapon, usually more than one, hidden all over her. Trickier in some of the couture clothing she preferred, especially the dresses.

Rather than take the hint, Marrok chuckled. "How do you do that?"

"Sleight of hand," she tossed back. After a pause, when neither of them said a word, Tala left him there to go collect her knives. "We should go back."

Not that she wanted to go back. Back to the watchful eyes and how every act, every decision, every word—or even if she did or said nothing—pissed someone off. Both packs seemed determined to fight this change with passive-aggressive resistance and a whole lot of bitching. But did the complainers step forward with a solution? Nope. Just left that for the alpha.

"I've got a better idea." Marrok cocked his head. "Let's go for a run."

Every cell in her body quickened at the idea. Other than a nightly solo run to check the perimeter, a habit she'd gotten into when she'd been one of the guards for her own pack, she hadn't had many opportunities to shift since her mating. Her wolf popped to her feet and snapped her teeth a couple times in eager anticipation.

Maybe a run was a good idea. Get some of this excess tension out of her system before going back at it. "Actually, that sounds lovely."

A playful grin lit his features. Immediately, Marrok started his shift, his body shimmering in the daylight, almost like seeing a mirage, as the shift pivoted around his soul, his innermost being, absorbing everything human about him to reveal the wolf.

Marrok, in wolf form, was impressive. More than that, but words escaped her. A pure black wolf with piercing blue eyes; the sheer size of him was enough to make most shifters hesitate to attack.

Lowering her gaze, Tala did the same, taking a deep breath then willing the change. Her body readjusted, spine realigning, along with shoulders, hips, elbows, knees. Technically, the process came with no sensation beyond a change in perspective, lower to the ground and pitched forward. But she swore her skin tingled every time the fur sprang forth in millions of tiny pinpricks.

Wolf in control for the moment, she lifted her face to the sun, enjoying the warmth, letting her senses reach out around her—feeling the solid earth under her paws, the breeze ruffling her fur, and the scent of...*her damn mate.*

• • •

His eager wolf practically burst from his body, forcing the shift faster than Marrok liked. He'd been wanting to play with Tala's wolf for weeks. Months even.

Taking her in now, he gave a happy wag of his tail. Tala was a lovely wolf, all white with gray socks and gray around her face, slender and lean, shorter than he and smaller by at least 30 percent. No wonder she had chosen to become a weapons expert as her preferred form of fighting. He'd seen her wolf before, of course, but they'd been busy with a battle against a werewolf at the time.

Marrok loosed a playful growl, bunching his muscles to pounce. But Tala turned on him, dropped her head, her ears flattened, and she exposed her teeth. A menacing growl, nothing like the playful one he'd issued, ripped from her throat.

What the hell?

"Tala?" He reached out with the telepathic connection all shifters shared when in animal form.

She didn't answer. Staying low to the ground, she inched forward, her threat clear. *Get away or pay with your life.*

Marrok stood his ground and did his best not to react to her aggression even as a reverberation of shock passed through him. He couldn't believe his mate was posturing to attack.

"Tala?" he tried again. *"Talk to me."*

With a suddenness that upped his shock to cannon-blast levels, she lunged. He turned in time to keep those deadly teeth from ripping out his throat.

His mate had gone mad.

He couldn't let her kill him. Marrok used his experience fighting in this form to twist around her. With a burst of strength and speed, he barreled into her side, knocking her to the ground. In a flash, he was on top of her. Using his greater bulk, he pinned her down. She went berserk, thrashing underneath him, snapping at him. Somehow—not easy with her snarling jaws and trying not to actually harm her—Marrok managed to get her neck between his teeth. He applied just enough pressure to force her to stillness, her sides heaving.

"Don't make me do this." He shoved the thought as hard as he could, hoping to get through.

It took forever. Tala had to be fighting her animal from inside, but the rage that could overcome a wolf shifter had clamped down on her like a vise, constricting her, snuffing out her humanity, and making it damn near impossible to shift back. Finally, the telltale shimmering hovered around her form, blurring her in his vision this close up.

Once she was human enough, Marrok released her and backed off, making the change himself.

Breathing hard, they stared at each other.

"What the hell was that, Tala?"

Her pale face reminded him of the moon—cold, remote, and unreachable. "I don't know. She took over completely. I could hear you and see what was happening, but I couldn't…" She shook her head. "I mean, she's been standoffish about you lately, but why would my wolf want to attack her mate?"

She might be playing it cool, but through their tenuous connection as mates, her panic was sharp.

Marrok's gut twisted. *Fuck.* "We'll figure it out. Okay?"

Chapter Two

Shaking was trying to consume her body. Tala pushed to her feet, stepping away from Marrok. She'd had to force her wolf into submission, almost like creating a box for that part of herself and shoving the wolf inside it, locking the door behind her. Even now, her animal was ripping at her mind, trying to break free.

Her wolf had never attacked anyone without Tala being in on the decision. *Never.*

Why now? Why their mate? Oh gods. Was this a sign that she'd made the wrong decision? That she shouldn't be here?

"She must be upset about earlier," she tried to reason.

Marrok stepped closer, but she stepped back. Until her wolf, who was scrambling against the inside of her head, calmed down, she didn't trust herself around him.

"In the meeting?"

She shook her head. "After."

He searched her expression then grimaced. "Let me guess. Sandalio?"

"Yes." Deep breath. Then another. "I'm being watched. His words."

A growl crawled out of his throat, his eyes flashing brilliant yellow, his wolf close to the surface, protective. As if he had any right to protect an alpha. He was part of the problem.

"*You* aren't helping any," she snapped.

Another grimace. "The medical staff thing?" he asked.

She crossed her arms with a glare.

He crossed his with an answering glare. "I thought we agreed that we need to move the combined packs here. We have more land and enough space for everyone."

The Banes territory spanned a few hundred acres. Over years of working together, they'd form what, to the outside world, appeared to be a town. A main complex where the alpha lived and where all meetings and business were carried out sat at the heart of the territory. Recently reconstructed, the modern glass building managed to fit seamlessly into the natural surroundings, but also stood out as a beacon of prosperity. On the back side they'd located all the training and weaponry. The pack's homes spread out from the front side, but still relatively close together. While the Canis pack's land was roughly the same size, they'd ended up widespread with no community center.

They'd agreed to move—

"I thought there'd be no more disagreeing with me in public."

"I wasn't disagreeing. I was pointing out what we'd already *agreed*."

Her wolf growled in her head, pacing and still unsettled, twisting nervous knots in Tala's stomach that she feared she'd never unravel.

What was with her? Before the mating, her inner beast had been all about Marrok and his wolf, practically begging for them.

Mate, Tala mentally chided.

Her wolf snapped her teeth, not having it.

Perhaps the animal side of her was feeding off Tala's own frustrated energy? Marrok, as a mate in the bedroom was… Even now her traitorous body yearned. Marrok as a mate out of the bedroom? If she had been born submissive, he also be fantastic.

But she wasn't. She was an alpha with a pack watching her every move, their every interaction. After the last month, her pack was far from impressed. Sign from the gods or no, she was losing their respect, one small decision at a time.

Unable to reconcile the opposing emotions buffeting her, Tala spun away to retrieve her knives. A growl rolled out of Marrok, and she spun to face him, hands on her hips.

"Did you growl at me?"

He had the grace to give a sheepish grimace, but at the same time managed to appear unapologetic. "Come back here. We're not done."

A command. Her traitorous body would have obeyed had the wolf inside her not leaped to attention and growled her fury. The deep rumble of it purred up Tala's throat.

Marrok's brows slammed down over his eyes. "What the hell, Tala?"

Did he really not get it?

Before she could set him straight, the high-pitched scream of a child pierced the quiet of the forest.

Knives forgotten, instinct had Tala sprinting, muscles burning with the speed, in the direction the scream had come from off to the right.

"Go along the river. I'll hit the woods," Tala yelled.

"Wait!" Marrok called.

She stopped mid-stride and spun to face her mate, who pointed. Following his direction, she discovered a mountain lion shifter slinking out of woods into the clearing where she stood, not fifty feet from her. No way had the cat shifter, notorious loners, not smelled or seen the evidence that it had wandered into pack territory.

Dammit.

Why the hell was this so damn hard at every single turn? Another predator shifter in their territory wouldn't help things with the members of their packs at all. This land was protected...by the alphas.

It swung its head, feral eyes glaring directly at her. Before she could yell out, silence settled over the area like someone hit a mute button, muffling any noise. Not a creature dared move or even breathe.

Anger seared her insides. Whatever this shifter had done to one of her people, he'd answer to Tala. Now.

She sprinted across the clearing, her wolf pushing her to superhuman speeds.

The mountain lion crouched, ready to pounce, and waited for her to come closer. Tala hesitated only a fraction at the fact that he didn't run—normally cougars didn't take on more than one wolf, especially not two alphas, because the odds were against them and they were smart. But not this shifter.

Tail whipping behind him, he prepared to fight. Only she had no intention of fighting that way.

Still running, Tala pulled one of the sticks out of her hair. From one of the many secret compartments on her vest, she produced a tiny blow dart and slipped it in the end of her weapon.

"Tala, no!"

Although she hadn't heard him behind or beside her, Marrok suddenly jumped between her and the cougar. She didn't stop fast enough and slammed into his outstretched hand. Her momentum flipped her sideways, and her face connected with the trunk of a tree with a sickening crack, the wood splintering under the impact. Nausea flooded her gut and crept up her throat as stars danced in her vision, competing with a blackness determined to consume her.

She dropped to the ground, shut her eyes, and sucked in a long slow breath, fighting the wave of unconsciousness. Finally, her head stopped buzzing. Forcing her eyes to open, she found Marrok kneeling over her, his face creased in concern.

"The cougar?" she asked, her head clearing quickly. Accelerated healing was one of the best bonuses of being a wolf shifter. She levered up and got her feet under her.

"He ran off."

"Dammit, Marrok. Why didn't you stop him?" Her wolf growled inside her head.

"I decided my mate, who I slammed against a tree, was too important." Real concern filled the words, but she was too focused on his actions.

She leveled a glare on him that would've had anyone in her own pack running for cover. "Speaking of which, why the hell did you get in my way?"

She could've leveled the cougar with one dart. The poison wouldn't kill a shifter but knock him out for hours. That's all they needed. Her wolf snarled and pushed against Tala's control, furious they'd been thwarted.

"My mate, still in human form, was going up against an already shifted mountain lion."

She shoved him in the chest, and irritation rose more as he didn't budge. "Your *alpha* mate."

An itching sensation in her eyes told her they'd changed as her wolf pushed harder. The metallic taste of blood dripped on her tongue as her canine teeth elongated in her mouth, and pricked lips shut tight around a multitude of expletives she held back. Pissed didn't begin to cover it.

Marrok scowled, but before he could comment, she stalked off into the woods. It was either that or snap his neck. Instead, she focused on making sure the child who'd screamed was safe.

Her mate followed in silence. Smart man. For once.

Chapter Three

Marrok was right behind Tala as she burst into a wider clearing beside the river to find a child of not more than seven crying, her dark hair hanging in her face. Despite confronting the cougar and stopping to argue about it, they were the first to get to her.

Where the fuck was the security on patrol in this area of his territory?

Tala slowed as she approached, obviously not wanting to scare the child. Deliberately Marrok hung back. Kids tended to be wary of him because of his size. That, and most alpha males weren't exactly approachable.

"Are you hurt?" Tala asked softly.

The child, one of his pack, stared back, tears slowing, and shook her head.

"Can I make sure?"

When the girl said nothing, Tala moved closer, crouching down, and gently checked her over. "Did he touch you?"

"No," came the whispered response.

Tala tossed Marrok a glance he easily interpreted as

"thank the gods." "Did he scare you?" she asked next.

That caused the tears to well back up in the girl's eyes.

"Oh sweetie," Tala gathered her close. "You're safe."

"Mira!" A frantic woman—Seela, who was a hunter for the pack—sprinted into the clearing and went straight for her daughter only to yank her from Tala's grasp, tossing a glare at his mate in a way that clearly said she wanted to singe the hairs off her head.

"What happened?" Seela asked her daughter. "Did this woman hurt you?"

Tala stepped back, her face going blank, but he didn't miss the way she paled.

"What the fuck did you just say?" Marrok snarled, the need to protect his mate overriding every other instinct and thought.

"Marrok," Tala muttered. A warning.

Seela turned her glare on him. "She's a *Canis*," she hissed.

"I'm your *alpha*," Tala snapped.

"You'll never—"

Marrok yanked Seela up by the arms, getting right in her face. "Because I respect you and your mate, I'll say this just once. Finish that sentence and you're out of the pack."

"Dammit, Marrok," Tala snapped. "Let her go."

With a growled warning at a now trembling Seela, he forced himself to do just that. Mira tugged on her mother's arm. After a moment of hesitation, she turned her head to the child.

"She saved me," Mira whispered. "From the mountain lion."

Seela's frown morphed and she flicked a glance brimming with confusion in Tala's direction, then knelt down to her daughter. "There was a cougar? On this land?"

Before Mira could do more than nod, more wolf shifters burst into the clearing, and the space turned into a circus for a hot minute.

"I don't give a shit if their union is blessed by the gods or not. Another shifter wouldn't have dared before the Canis pack came here," someone muttered, but soft enough that he couldn't pinpoint who. By the stiffening of her shoulders, Tala heard, too.

"Aaron," Marrok snapped at one of the guards posted nearest this spot. "Take three men and go after the cougar to make sure he's out of our territory."

"Sir." Aaron ran off to execute the order.

Tala stepped slightly ahead of Marrok, a subtle show of dominance. "Until we know if this is an isolated incident, we will step up security protocols. Go back to your homes until we communicate things are in place."

That mountain lion might be only the beginning. What if other shifters who wanted their territory viewed the pack—still divided, both physically and because of dissent over their mating—as weak?

"What about tonight?" someone called out.

Full moon tonight. Fuck. "The moon must be honored," Marrok assured them.

Only to receive a flat-lipped glare from Tala. Through their connection, all he got was anger. What had he done now?

With a barely concealed roll of her eyes, she stalked away.

Irritation scraping over his skin, setting the hairs on end, Marrok followed. "What did I say?" he asked as he drew abreast of her. "You think we should cancel the celebration?"

She flicked him a glance. "It's not what you said. It's that you didn't even glance at me for a confirmation first."

Okay. Fair point. He was having trouble correcting years of habit and being the only one in charge. She'd already pointed this out several times. Still, that hadn't exactly been a big thing to make a decision over.

"And do *not* threaten your people over me," Tala snarled next.

That's how she'd seen that? "I was protecting my—"

"I can fucking speak for myself. Thanks."

Marrok blew out a sharp breath. "I'm not going to apologize for instinct. You're my mate, alpha or not. I can't *not* defend you."

"You won't even try, you mean."

That was not what he meant. "Tala—"

She snapped up a hand. "We'll discuss this later." They'd reached the main building that housed the room where they'd be meeting with the fighters.

A low chuff of frustration came from his wolf. Marrok echoed the sentiment. He couldn't change who he essentially was, and neither of them had figured her out yet. "For someone who doesn't like being overridden, you sure like to give orders."

On that note, he held the glass door open for her, giving a sarcastic wave for her to precede him into the slick black granite foyer, which no doubt he'd pay for later.

This wasn't exactly easy for him, either.

The meeting with their fighters only continued the shitshow, a reflection of the frustration both alphas and both packs were feeling. All were worried that this one cougar represented a greater threat. A sign that other supernaturals considered the combined pack to be weaker. An early warning shot of things to come.

Finally, hours into it, Marrok leaned over to Tala. "I feel we should all go get ready for the full moon. Do you agree?"

She stiffened in her seat. "Yes."

Together they stood. "You know what to do for tonight," Marrok said. They'd already agreed on increased patrols on a rotating basis. "We'll resume the unfinished topics tomorrow."

Not looking at him, Tala muttered, "Astra should be here by now. I promised her I'd get ready with her and take her to the celebration."

That's right. Her sister, who had remained on Canis land any time Tala was here, acting as alpha in her stead, had come to visit for his and Tala's first full moon since their mating night.

"Fine," he said.

Tala nodded, still not looking at him, then walked away.

Marrok held his own annoyance behind a dam he'd built up over years, trained from childhood as the obvious next in line for alpha. An emotional alpha was a weak alpha. But damned if his mate didn't have his emotions dangling on a rope.

There had to be some way through for two alphas leading a combined pack of enemies.

Chapter Four

The full moon celebrations lasted all night, and this was the last damn place she wanted to be. Tala's cheeks ached from holding her smile in place. She resisted the urge to rub her tired eyes, made worse by the smoke rising from the massive crackling bonfire. Her pretty blue sundress, the color of Marrok's eyes, was now saturated with the scent of campfire.

At least the mark on her face from when Marrok essentially shoved her into that tree was gone. What had been a baseball-sized bruise on her cheek had been smaller and reduced to green rather than black and purple by the time she'd gone to Astra's room to dress. Thank the gods for accelerated healing. Likely even that was gone by now.

Right in time for the party she didn't want to attend.

Wolf shifters celebrated every full moon—or more accurately, their ancient history, through the lineage of werewolf ancestors, of being held in its thrall, though they could now shift at will—with a night of revelry held deep in the wilderness. Wisely, she and Marrok hadn't allowed anyone to shift, deeming it too dangerous yet for both packs to shift together. Relations needed to improve before that happened. Instead they'd hunted in separate groups earlier and come together to cook their prizes over open fires. Astra had also brought beer and fixings for s'mores. A small gesture of friendship Tala appreciated.

Exhaustion hung heavy over Tala's body. Gods, she was dragging like a swimmer caught in a riptide.

Marrok stood across the clearing from her. Usually glued to her side, he seemed to have read the giant *Give Me Space* sign practically written in neon across her forehead.

Tala turned her attention away, gazing around the meadow, beautiful in the full moonlight. Such a setting was idyllic, as wolf shifters preferred to surround themselves with nature. The full moon, the rhythms their ancestors used to be tied to, radiated a cool, calming glow over everything. A night for celebration.

That was, if they didn't all kill one another first.

"No bloodshed." She whispered the prayer to any gods listening. She lifted her gaze to the moon with a particular plea for those goddesses.

"What'd you say?" Her sister's voice broke into her plea.

Tala winced. Damn wolf shifter hearing. "Nothing."

"Yeah, right." Though Tala had moved apart from the others, needing a minute to herself, her sly sister had snuck close and now stood beside Tala, peering at the wolf shifters around them. "Do you think it would help if I slept with one of the Banes? As a gesture of goodwill, of course? They do have a tasty selection of male wolves."

"Astra," she hissed.

In response, Astra wiggled her provocative backside, covered in a pale turquoise dress that barely covered her ass, and continued as though she hadn't been warned. "Marrok looks particularly fuck-worthy tonight. You lucky girl."

"Gods save me." Tala dropped to sit on a felled tree,

using it as a bench of sorts.

Astra sat beside her. "Tala Canis Banes, you can't tell me you don't want your mate. I've seen the way you look at him."

Terrific. Tala lifted a shoulder in a shrug.

Astra shook her head, returning to her perusal of the gathered shifters. "I'd be all over that tall hunk of man-cake if I were you," she muttered. "I'm surprised your wolf isn't dry humping him every second of the day."

"Lower your voice."

Astra hooted. "If a man looked at me the way he looks at you, I'd spontaneously multiple-orgasm."

"Orgasms aren't the problem," Tala snapped, making sure to whisper, not wanting to be overheard.

A wicked smile graced her sister's features. "I'm glad to hear it."

Her wolf, meanwhile, snarled in her head.

Dammit.

Sandalio walked by where they sat, nodding at them both, but with a face like he'd smelled something rotten.

Astra flipped him off behind his back as he moved away. "He's going to cause problems," she warned.

"Welcome to a show already in progress," Tala muttered.

Marrok glanced over, gaze glittering in a way she now recognized, and her traitorous body leaped in response.

Tala uncrossed and recrossed her legs, trying to ease the ache of desire, then scowled at the action. She didn't fidget. Alphas couldn't afford to fidget—it made them appear nervous. A nervous alpha was a dead alpha.

Apparently, she didn't do a great job hiding it, because Astra sent her a smirk. "Got an itch you can't scratch?"

Unamused, Tala let loose a soft snarl of warning. Astra held up her hands. "Sorry. Too soon?"

"Maybe I should find you a mate so you can enjoy it and tell me what you think."

"Hell no. A mate is the last thing I'm interested in." Astra shuddered.

Me, too. Only the thought didn't hold the conviction it once had. Which made no sense. This mating was arranged, for the benefit of the packs. She didn't love Marrok. She respected him. Needed him to make this truce work. She could even admit that her desire for the man had turned into a heady, uncontrollable urge, a need only he could assuage. That was just physical.

Nothing more.

Her wolf turned up her nose, taunting. Calling Tala all kinds of liar.

She couldn't help glancing in her mate's direction again. As she watched, a child, no older than five or six, approached him.

Tala tensed. Most wolf shifter males, especially alphas, couldn't be bothered with children. She'd seen kids get snapped at, growled at, even cuffed or shoved, for approaching their alpha. Look at how, earlier today, he'd stood back and let her deal with the child frightened by the cougar shifter.

This child wasn't part of the Canis pack, but Tala wouldn't let anything happen. Intending to intercept, she started to her feet, only to stumble to a halt. Instead of scaring her, Marrok knelt down to the little girl's level and listened to her with all the focus he afforded any adult wolf shifter.

Unable to turn away, Tala observed how the girl, obviously one of his pack, had no fear of her alpha. After several long minutes of earnest conversation, the girl giggled. Shock sizzled through Tala, and her mouth went dry as Marrok chuckled and tapped his cheek. The child gave him a sweet kiss before she ran off into the night.

Astra appeared at her side. "Those pheromones must be set on boil."

Tala peeled her eyes from her mate with difficulty.

"What?" Then she shook her head. "That's only during the mating. It's been weeks."

Astra gave her a pointed look, one she recognized from playing tricks on the elders as kids. One that meant her next words were a ruse. "That's the word. But it makes sense that they'd last longer after *your* mating, because you're both alphas. Your heart could start its own drumline about now. I'm turned on just standing next to you."

Holy hellhounds! Astra was right. Her heart beat a strong tattoo against her ribs.

She *never* allowed herself to show inner turmoil in public. *Never.* With more effort than the ability typically took, she forced her heart to calm. What a chump. Here she was all worked up over her mate treating a child with kindness. Granted, she'd never seen anything like that with other alphas. Didn't mean she needed to go all gushy on him.

What was wrong with her?

Thank heaven for Astra, who'd covered brilliantly. She'd mock-whispered the words, but loud enough that those around them could hear perfectly. Attributing Tala's reaction to the mating call was quick thinking.

"When is it supposed to wear off, anyway?" Tala grumbled, playing along.

Astra laughed. "With that as my mate"—she nodded to Marrok—"I wouldn't want it to." She turned an assessing eye on Tala. "Especially given the glow you've picked up."

"I am *not* glowing," Tala muttered between clenched teeth.

Marrok glanced their way, a knowing smirk playing around his mouth.

"I think he heard you." Tala turned her head to hiss the words. A glance at her mate told her he now watched them openly. As soon as he caught her gaze, he gave a sexy-as-all-get-out wink. Damn the man. How could he have her body leaping with anticipation with a silly wink? Especially when she was still mad at him?

With powerful strides he came around the fire to where she stood, and Tala remained where she was, rooted to the spot, unable to look away.

"Astra," he greeted.

"Brother." Astra glanced between them. "You two might want to go bleed off some of the sexual tension."

Marrok choked a laugh at that and finally turned his gaze to her sister.

With a tip of her chin, Astra indicated several couples rushing into the cover of darkness and trees.

Oh, hell. Everyone could feel that? Feel their rising desire? She'd heard of the alpha couples' emotions having a direct impact on the pack but had never experienced that herself. Was that what this was?

Astra must've caught the gist of Tala's thoughts because she shrugged. "Yeah. I'm almost in pain standing this close to you. In fact, I'm thinking I might go see if that tall drink of yummy across the way wants to play."

Marrok glanced in the direction Astra was looking. "You don't want to mess with Rafe."

Astra pouted. "I'm not going to *mess* with him, brother dear, I'm going to *play* with him."

"He doesn't play nice."

Tala held back a groan. Worst possible thing Marrok could've said to her bad-boy-loving sister.

"Goody." Astra pursed her lips suggestively.

Marrok covered his mouth with his hand to smother a laugh. "You've been warned."

Astra tipped her head and stared at the man until he happened to glance up, stilling as he caught sight of her. She sent him a saucy smile, but instead of going over to Rafe, she wandered off into the night, leaving Tala and Marrok alone together.

Tala turned to her mate, trying to keep her heart steady and her face without emotion—until she encountered deep blue eyes crinkled at the corners as though he could read her thoughts. Was he struggling, too?

Marrok ran a hand down her arm in a brief, almost comforting, caress. Since the mating, he'd done this a lot, as though he couldn't stop touching her—not overtly, just constant contact. Her body itched to touch him back in the same manner, but her wolf held her back.

What's with *you?* Tala prodded. But the fickle creature yawned and turned away, shutting Tala out. She ignored her animal side and focused instead on her mate.

Her mate who watched her, an oddly intent light in his eyes. If she hadn't known better, she'd say concern had replaced amusement, darkening the color. At her confused frown, he smiled, and Tala found herself distracted by the crinkles around his eyes. Laugh lines she found seriously sexy when combined with that knockout grin of his. And when he was kind, like now, she could lose her heart to that sexy, sweet side of him.

But none of that changed the fact that his behavior was losing her the Canis pack.

She glowered. Her alpha mate was going to have to learn to share soon, and consult with her, and allow her to be alpha half the time, or she would have to make him.

His eyes flickering in the firelight, he stared at her, and she stared back. He held out a hand. "Join me in the woods?"

Tala knew what he was asking. She licked her lips and shifted on her feet. She shouldn't.

He leaned forward, lips by her ear. "Yes. You should."

Tala gasped, though only Marrok caught it. *Probably.* How had he known?

A quick check told her the rest of the gathering weren't

paying them any attention. For once. Damn her body and damn him for being nice to that little girl. The sight had left her panting. Even her wolf had perked up for a second, tail twitching.

Hiding a deep breath, Tala put her hand in his and allowed him to lead her out of the circle of warmth and light cast by the fire into the cooler, darker night beyond.

Every cell of her being focused on her mate, Tala was ready and willing for what he had in mind. They wound their way through the pine trees, the fresh, spicy scent surrounding them. A good distance from the revelers, Marrok slowed and pulled her softly into his arms, his body wrapping her in warmth, hard against hers. He lowered his head, and she lifted her lips, eager for his kiss.

"I hate that we fight," he murmured against the corner of her mouth.

Words guaranteed to soften her heart. "I—"

A shout rose up from the people they'd just left, angry and getting louder by the second.

Chapter Five

Tala rushed into the clearing and around the bonfire to where every person present had gathered. Marrok followed closely behind as she pushed her way to the center of the circle of snarling wolf shifters. At least no one had changed.

There, sitting on a log, tears streaming down her face, was Accalia. Just her freakin' luck. The woman was of the Canis pack and had an uncanny ability to make trouble. She also had a penchant for lies and drama.

"What happened?" Tala demanded.

Accalia pointed at a man from the Banes pack, her face twisted with distaste. "He tried to kill me."

For his part the man let loose a low growl, which set off a chain of low growls like a stone cast into a pond sending ripples over the surface. "I sure as hell didn't," he denied.

Shit. This was going downhill fast, and Tala was already in a rough position. "Do you have injuries needing treatment?"

Accalia turned that hateful glare her way. "You don't believe me?"

"That's not what I said. I want to make sure any urgent

injuries are treated immediately." As far as she could tell, other than a ripped dress and her tears, Accalia was fighting-fit.

Accalia's expression turned sulky. "No." She narrowed her eyes. "I demand that wolf pay the price immediately. We are in neutral territory and have been forbidden by you to shift."

"We will make an investigation, of course." Marrok stepped closer to Tala.

Dammit. Why couldn't the man have held off for two seconds and let her deal with this?

Tala turned her own glare on her mate, who showed no reaction, except a small flare of irritation she barely caught. Did he seriously have zero clue what a horrible position he'd put her in with her pack? Or was he playing dumb?

Of course, she agreed with Marrok's call, but his unilateral decision forced her into a "her pack versus his pack" situation—she could protect her pack member from the Banes, or side with her mate condemning one of her own pack. Given her tenuous hold on her people, nothing could be worse.

Deliberately, Tala held her tongue.

Accalia was a drama queen and a liar, but her timing tonight felt off. Tala's gut instinct told her a hidden player was involved here, and she meant to discover who. Her wolf stood on alert, hackles raised.

"What do you say, Alpha?" From beyond the flickering light of the flames, Sandalio stepped forward, the gathering parting for him.

Despite his age, the wolf shifter still made an intimidating figure of a man. Tall, almost as tall as Marrok, and leanly muscled. Tala always mentally labeled him as wiry. His form of fighting was more that of a fox—quick and sneaky—than a wolf. He stood straight and proud, oozing the prowess his many years boasted. Only his salt-and-pepper hair and wrinkled skin gave away his age.

She should have known he would be behind this. He'd been biding his time to move on her as alpha since she took over the role.

Tala crossed her arms. "We will conduct an investigation."

"No!" Accalia jumped to her feet, holding up the tattered bodice of her dress with one hand. "I want him punished now."

Tala glanced at the man accused. His eyes glowed in the flicker of the firelight as he held his change in check, his chest heaving with the effort. Wisely, he said nothing. Tala stood her ground and kept her heart rate even. "If the investigation determines him guilty, then he will be."

Accalia's eyes bugged. "If?" she screeched. "Are you calling me a liar?"

"I'm saying an investigation will be held first."

"Is that how things will go now that our clans have been joined?" Sandalio spit into the fire, the hiss fizzing in the thick silence following his question. "The Banes Alpha will decide everything for both packs, while the Canis Alpha meekly bows to his command? Was that sign from the gods even real?"

Shit.

"I commanded nothing," Marrok snarled. His low voice reverberated with his authority and power. Even Tala's wolf winced.

Sandalio turned to the crowd and held up his arms theatrically. "Even now he speaks, and she listens. This is why a female alpha was never a good—"

"If you're going to challenge me, old man, get on with it." Tala's quietly spoken words cut him off as effectively as a scream.

"Tala," Marrok muttered. She silenced him with a glance

so full of fury, even he knew to shut up.

Sandalio slowly pivoted to face her. "We both know a strong leader is what is needed now. Not our rival's bitch."

Tala gave a bored sigh. "Was that a challenge? I couldn't tell."

She pushed deliberately. If she didn't end this now, he would undermine her leadership, and now her mating, every step of the way.

"You want me to challenge you?"

"I'm still waiting for you to have the balls you claim are necessary for the job. Either challenge me or shut the hell up."

That did it. The crowd scattered, pushing back and out of the way as Sandalio shimmered, signaling his change. Tala kept her eyes glued to him. Some shifters took longer than others to shift, some were quicker. The realigning and elongating of bones was smooth and easy if done slowly, more jarring if quick, but over time supposedly became less jarring and therefore easier to move fast.

"Tala, shift!" Marrok yelled.

She ignored the order. "You do anything to interfere, mate, and I'll rip your throat out myself."

Not removing her gaze from her opponent—attacking before the change was complete when the fight involved a challenge was deemed bad form—she knew without looking that Marrok got the message. His thundering growl told her he did and silenced everyone else.

Sandalio shook his head and the fuzziness disappeared, his form coming into sharp relief, the final phase of the shift, signaled the time to fight. Before her, where a tough old man had challenged her, now stood a massive wolf. Dark gray fur covered his body, with lighter gray around his eyes and snout. Sandalio stood larger than most.

Even while he made the change, she mentally took stock

of what she had available to use against him, using her sleight of hand skills to slip one of the few weapons she'd bothered to bring into her palm.

Tala never shifted for a fight. As a female wolf she was smaller, physically outmatched, but while she was more vulnerable as a human, she was also more adept and able to use weapons. The problem was, Sandalio had seen her fight several battles to become alpha, but she'd never seen him fight in his wolf form. A disadvantage she'd have to deal with quickly.

Without an ounce of hesitation, she ran straight at the wolf shifter. As she came in range, he lunged, snapping his jaws, but she slid like a base runner coming into home, between his legs and under his belly.

She used the Kubotan she'd slipped from her pocket earlier like a baton of sorts. As she slid by, she jabbed the end of the hard instrument into the wrist joint above Sandalio's forefoot, using her momentum for added heft. A satisfying pop signaled she'd done damage.

See how he did with one foot hobbled now.

A cloud of dust followed Tala as she pushed to her feet, making it hard to see, the itch of it inside her lungs annoying but not debilitating.

Immediately, she ducked under Sandalio's head. He'd whirled on her faster than she expected, and his razor-sharp teeth barely missed her, his breath hot on her back. Rather than put distance between them, Tala hooked her right arm around his neck, grabbing a hank of fur for purchase, and swung up onto his back. There she slammed her heels in, like a cowboy spurring a horse, only the three-inch heels of her stilettos did a hell of a lot more damage as they pierced his skin and stabbed into his ribs.

Marrok had teased her for wearing those shoes in the woods.

Sandalio howled and jerked under her, curling back on his body. She tried to pull her foot free, only the heel stayed buried. Pain lanced up her leg as the wolf's teeth sunk deep. With a heave, he slung her off his back and slammed her into the rough trunk of a nearby pine tree.

Tala's vision went black as she lay crumpled on the ground, pine needles raining down on her from above, filling her senses with the woodsy scent that made her think of her mate. In a haze she could hear Marrok yelling her name and others shouting at him. They had to be holding him back.

This was her fucking fight. Even if he didn't get it, everyone else would.

But Tala wasn't focused on her mate, or her pain, or her lack of vision, which would clear shortly. Instead, she kept her eyes closed and used her phenomenal hearing, totally attuned to the soft tread of Sandalio's paws on the ground, moving ever closer. He would go for the easy kill. The way she had fallen, her throat was exposed...perfect bait.

"At last..." His thought reached her, though she doubted he meant it to.

He leaned over her now, his stinky dog breath hot on her face. *Do it already, you coward,* she silently willed him.

With a snarl, he reared back. As he went for the kill, Tala moved with the speed of a rattlesnake strike. She snatched one of her specially made metal sticks out of the long pocket along her thigh and jammed it, pointy end first, into Sandalio's neck, though she avoided the artery.

The sharp instrument plunged deep, and the wolf shifter dropped to the ground beside her. The metallic scent of blood spilled into the air as his wound seeped, red staining the earth beside him. The injury wouldn't kill him but would take him out for several days as he healed.

Tala stayed on the ground, her leg pinned under Sandalio's greater weight.

Gathering the will to imbue the words, she spoke with force and controlled fury to those gathered. "Half an inch down and he'd be dead. Because of my respect for his age and all he's done for the Canis pack in the past, I have decided to show mercy. However, he and his kin will find a new pack. Immediately."

Chapter Six

After a long moment of shock held them all immobile when Tala came out the victor, those of his pack who held Marrok back released him. He'd lost his shit when he thought his mate was about to be killed, and four of his strongest wolves still hadn't been entirely enough. His wolf had been frantic inside his head, lending added power to his limbs while at the same time pushing to be released so he could rip out the bastard's throat who threatened their mate.

Now he shoved the unconscious mass of the wolf Tala had defeated away from her to pull her into his arms. "Tala? Talk to me. Are you—"

She shoved him off her. Hard. "I'm fine," she spat.

His wolf managed to growl and whimper at the same time. Something was wrong with their mate. Marrok held up his hands. He watched as she gingerly rose to her feet, giving her head a shake. Then he, too, moved to his feet.

Rather than address him, Tala turned a hard stare on Accalia, who now cowered on the ground. His magnificent mate stalked to the she-wolf and crouched down. In a voice all the more deadly for the softness, she addressed every person listening.

"There will be an investigation. If your alleged attacker is found guilty, he will be punished. If it is found you have lied, you will join Sandalio."

Accalia paled so drastically, Marrok wondered if she'd pass out.

"Do you want to rethink your charges?" Tala asked.

Accalia started to shake. "He didn't attack me," she said through pale, pinched lips. "Sandalio helped me fake it."

"Was anyone else involved?" Tala asked.

Accalia's hair fell into her eyes as she shook her head, her gaze lowered. "Not that I know of."

Tala rose to her feet and surveyed the gathering. "Any other challengers tonight?" She asked the question almost conversationally. Like she was asking if anyone wanted more to eat. Damn, she was magnificent.

"No?" Tala asked. A long silence greeted her question. "Good."

She took a deep breath, and the next words came out in a raised voice. "I believe we've celebrated this full moon enough. Time to get to the business of learning to live together as one pack. In peace."

She turned to him and held out her hand. "Shall we?"

Marrok grinned, unable to hold back his pride in his mate, and took her hand. His wolf still wanted to check that she was unharmed, but he suspected he'd lose a limb if he tried.

Together they walked out of the clearing, leaving the business of cleaning up to the others. They made the trek through the woods to their home in silence.

As soon as they entered their suite, Tala went to stand in front of the long mirror in the bathroom and pulled back the blue skirt of her dress to reveal a nasty scrape up her thigh, probably from when she'd slid under Sandalio. She also inspected the bite on her foot. He should've carried her out of the forest. She hadn't even limped.

Marrok couldn't cage his wolf's growl at the sight.

Tala shoved her dress down to spin around and bare her teeth, her canines elongating as she growled back, louder and longer.

A much louder, much deeper growl reverberated from him in answer. "I've had about all I can take with you growling at me today," he snapped. "I was *concerned*."

She didn't pull her teeth in, instead leaning casually against the counter, arms crossed, and lifted a single unimpressed brow. "Oh?"

What? He couldn't even be concerned for his mate now? Not even in private?

He stepped closer, wolf pushing him to show her what he meant, though he didn't bare his teeth in return. "In my pack, growling at the alpha is a challenge, and baring your teeth is asking for a fight."

"What if that alpha is being a jackass?"

Marrok's head snapped back as if she'd struck him. "I was worried for my mate. Is that wrong?"

That only earned him a glare. "Have any of your people pulled you aside to tell you you're not being alpha enough? Or challenged you directly for mating me?"

His brows snapped down over his eyes. This again? "No."

"Maybe that's because you're *still* acting like the *only* alpha in this equation."

Now Marrok crossed his arms, imitating her closed-off body posture. "You're my mate. You were in a fight. I was fucking *worried*, Tala."

Terrified more like. Frantic. That's what she did to him.

Tala snorted. "Which is exactly the problem. You shouldn't have been worried. You, out of everyone there, should have been the *least* worried. I'm every inch the alpha you are, and I *earned* my place, rather than inherited it."

Marrok stared at his mate, anger and frustration boiling over, triggering a response that was a damn sight more unnerving—pure, unadulterated need.

Fuck.

He couldn't peel his gaze away. Her green eyes glowed with anger and power, and her teeth sharpened. Her wolf pushing at her should've had him on high alert, but her breasts strained against her vest, nipples erect and begging for his attention. Meanwhile her heart rate was slow and steady, in complete control. And the alpha waves she was giving off, clotting the air, were about the sexiest damn things he'd ever come across. That familiar heavy pulsing shot blood straight to his groin. He'd never been this hard, even in his youth.

Dammit.

Before he could say a word, Tala whipped off the thin gold chain around her waist and snapped it at him. One end of the device coiled around his neck—not too tight, a warning. A demonstration. He winced at the bite of the sting, and he had to tense against the instinctive need to defend himself. Instead, he held still.

So her belt was a whip of some sort? She was always pulling random weapons out of thin air like that. Where the hell did she keep them all?

Despite it being wrong on every level, he wanted her. Tala was fucking incredible, and he needed to claim her. Now. The musky scent of her arousal told him she was equally turned on.

His mate wanted to be in charge? Okay by him. "Prove it."

Her shoulders stiffened and her eyes narrowed. "What?"

"Show me just how alpha you can be."

He could see the battle in her eyes. She was angry with him. Angrier with herself for wanting him right now. The second she made her decision, he knew, because her heart rate took off.

She led him by the chain around his neck to the bed, and he went meekly enough. His wolf watched warily, not liking that they were essentially trapped, but also caught up in the desire to claim. At the bed, she spun them both around. With a none-too-gentle shove to the middle of his chest, she toppled him onto the bed. Before he knew it, she was straddling his hips. The chain was off his neck, but before he could touch her, she bound his wrists to the headboard. The coils of the whip wound tighter when he tugged against them.

His wolf growled low inside his head, but no urge to shift and protect himself came over him. At the same time, his cock swelled.

Tala made quick work of his belt and zipper and peeled his pants down his body, tossing them on the floor. Before he had any clue what she was up to, with no teasing or warning, she wrapped her mouth around him and sucked hard.

Marrok practically came off the bed. A groan ripped out of his throat as she took him deep, surrounding his shaft with heat and pressure and...fuck she looked so beautiful. She pulled back, releasing him with a pop, but then ran her tongue up and down his shaft, circling the head each time. Then back into her mouth. He moved his hips, and she let him pump in and out of her. Faster and faster. Before he could explode inside her, however, she released him, a wicked grin on those now swollen lips.

"*Tala.*" His wolf howled inside his head.

She ignored his plea as she slowly slipped her dress over her head, then discarded her bra. The sight of her pink-tipped breasts about sent him over the edge. Then she shoved off him to stand beside the bed and shimmied out of her panties. Every inch of her delectable body was uncovered, and every nerve in his body throbbed and strained for her. The coils around his arms tightened, holding him fast.

She straddled his legs again, but not where he wanted her. He bucked, trying to make her move higher.

Tala grinned. "Do you want to touch me?"

"You know I do."

Her eyes widened at the wolf-roughed timbre of his voice, obviously aware of the edge he rode. The change rippled under his skin, but he held it back.

"Where?" she asked.

He swallowed, and his eyes dropped of their own accord.

"Here?" she purred. She raised her own hands to knead her breasts. She tossed her head back as she plucked at her nipples with her fingers.

"*Tala.*" Her name ripped out of his throat.

She lifted her head. "More?"

He doubted he could take much more.

"Maybe here?" While keeping one hand on her breast, she trailed the other down her flat belly to the apex of her thighs.

A small whimper escaped her as she touched herself.

Ours, his wolf snapped in his head.

"Stop," Marrok demanded. As much as it turned him on to watch her, giving her pleasure was his right as her mate. He should be the one touching her.

Those gorgeous green eyes twinkled at him. "Or what?"

Did she just challenge him? He'd show her who was in charge now. With all the strength his form afforded, he strained against the bindings until the chain dug painfully into his skin. What had she tied him up with?

He was so focused on breaking free so he could show his mate who was boss, he didn't notice her moving until she sank onto his shaft in one long stroke. His body jerked under her and he stopped struggling, his entire attention on what she was doing.

Tala continued to touch her own body as she rode him— her strokes long, deep, and torturously slow. In that instant, he and his wolf forgot the need to dominate, too wrapped up in the sensuous moves of her body, the erotic image of her hands as they played across her skin, and the sensation of every motion as she fucked him.

Gradually she increased the pace. Her lips fell apart as she panted her need, her own release as close as his. Suddenly, she opened her eyes and pinned him with a look that was pure alpha.

"Now," she commanded.

Damned if his body didn't obey, his orgasm slamming through him in waves. At the same time, she screamed as her body clamped around, milking his cock. Tala continued to ride him as the waves crested through them both over and over, easing until they collapsed together, their ragged breathing the only sound in the room.

With languorous movements, she reached up, and with barely a touch, the coils unwound from his arms. He needed to ask her where she got that thing. She lay her head on his chest, and he wrapped his arms around her, both he and his wolf oddly content, despite the fact that another alpha had dominated them both.

The conversation was far from over. He knew that. But, for now, he and his mate rested quietly, bodies still intimately connected.

An unfamiliar warmth built inside him—happiness and satisfaction mixed with something else, though he couldn't quite put his finger on what. A deeper emotion he was strangely reluctant to identify. Certainly a sensation he'd never fully experienced. His wolf gave a pleased hum as Tala curled into him more.

His mate certainly kept him on his toes—alpha in charge one second, vulnerable woman in his arms the next.

He pulled her closer and shut his eyes. They'd figure out the rest later.

Chapter Seven

Sun stole through the blinds, illuminating their room. Marrok rolled over in bed, reaching for Tala only to find her side empty, the mattress still warm under his fingertips, her wildflower scent all over him.

With a frown, he propped himself up on one elbow. "Tala?"

His answer was the *click* of the bathroom door lock followed by the hiss of the shower. Nothing about that should have tipped him off, but Marrok's wolf went on alert. Not pacing, but ears pricked and focused entirely on that door and the woman behind it.

Unable to just lie in bed, Marrok got up and dressed quickly, all the while his mind churning over what had happened yesterday and last night. Another *click* had him turning to face the bathroom. Tala emerged dressed, her usual elegant self in black slacks and a frilly white blouse, a different pair of stilettos on her feet, and hair pulled back in a knot at the base of her skull. Not a weapon in sight, except that gold belt again. It appeared so innocuous in its present form around her waist.

He knew different.

Without a word or glance his way, his mate moved to the wardrobe, where she pulled out her large suitcase and hefted it onto the bed, which squeaked its protest. Still ignoring him, Tala pulled a hunk of clothes out of her closet and started carefully and meticulously packing.

Marrok…was not entirely sure how to deal with this.

She didn't pause as he stood there like a useless ass and watched. "I think we're going about this wrong," she said. "Pushing too fast. I will send half my people to live in your territory for the next six months. The weaker half. You send me yours."

His wolf paced in his head as Marrok crossed his arms. Somehow, he knew a kicker was coming. "Sounds like a plan. Mix everyone up in both territories."

She didn't look his way, simply continued with her task.

"And where will we stay? Part time at your place and part time at mine?" he asked.

"I'll stay at my place." Now she stopped packing and looked him directly in the eye. "If you want a place in my bed, you'll have to earn it."

If he didn't know better, he'd swear the pit in his stomach was panic. Tala meant what she said. He didn't need instinct or the still flimsy mating bond connecting them to realize that on his own.

Dammit. He'd hoped maybe the connection developing between them in the bedroom—just last night, she'd allowed him to hold her through the night after sex that had stolen his reason and will—might have helped outside the bedroom. Not fixed things, exactly, but soothed their issues.

His wolf raised his hackles. So did Marrok. The urge to cross the room and get in her space battled with common sense. The anger pouring off his mate in waves kept him where he was.

He'd witnessed firsthand what she could do in a fight. He knew better than to piss her off more. Instead he crossed his arms and planted his feet wide. She'd have to get around him to leave. "Is this about the alpha thing?"

Her hands paused in her task. "The alpha thing," she muttered, more to herself. Then straightened to shoot him an unimpressed glare. "Yeah. It's about the alpha thing."

Anger bubbled up over his panic. "Have you disagreed with any of my decisions?"

Emotion darkened her eyes to emerald, and her shoulders fell before she turned back to her packing. "That's not the point," she said quietly.

The disappointment lacing her voice was like a spike to the heart. This was on him. He knew that. But none of his actions, not one, were intended to cause problems. They came from who he was as alpha and as a mate. He tried to be respectful, take her into account, make sure his decisions were fair. Any time he thought she might disagree, he discussed it with her. They couldn't discuss every fucking little thing. They'd get nowhere that way. Was that really what she wanted?

"I thought… Maybe after last night…" He ran a hand through his hair.

A flash of regret disappeared behind a wall of steel in her eyes. "Great sex doesn't fix everything. Sometimes, it's just sex."

Just sex? That was it for her? What the fuck was he supposed to do now? No one had ever found him lacking his entire life. Marrok opened and shut his mouth, unable to process his reaction. He was a proven alpha. He'd made decisions, and he wouldn't apologize for that. What's more, he'd protected his mate. Or tried to.

Before he could form a response, Tala's cell phone rang.

Her expression showed zero surprise as she picked it up.

His extra-sensitive hearing picked up Astra's voice on the other end. "I got your text."

"And you're ready to go?"

"The car will be here in twenty."

"I'll meet you there."

She was leaving now? Before they had a chance to talk about it? No. Just hell no.

Tala moved away, though she kept her gaze trained on him warily. Hurt and disappointment joined shock and fury. His mate didn't trust him. Maybe didn't want him. Marrok's wolf, who'd been silently watching, now raised his head and howled. The empty sound was a pure reflection of Marrok's own reaction.

He had done this.

Fix, his wolf insisted.

Marrok agreed, determination wrapped around all the other emotions bombarding him. He had to fix this.

At the same time, he had no doubt he couldn't make her stay. Marrok turned away and closed his eyes, reaching for a calm so elusive, it felt as though he was trying to hold sand in a sieve. But he had to do something.

Think, dammit. How could he find some way to connect with his mate? Get them on the same side? Them against both their respective packs?

The world around him stilled with the thought.

When did it turn into me against my pack?

The question hit square in the chest, robbing him of the ability to breathe right for a few long seconds. Because he knew exactly when. Love hadn't been a part of the bargain for them, but suddenly, he couldn't imagine his life without her in it.

I love her.

He didn't know when Tala had captured his heart. The

strong, independent, fierce woman who hid beneath a façade of icy control and couture clothing had won him, heart and soul. All the signs had been there—his wolf's approval of her, his need to claim, to protect, to care for a woman who pushed him away at every turn. Despite their obvious physical connection, which couldn't be all pheromones, he had no idea if love even made her radar. Worse, if the troubles she had with her pack were any evidence, "worthy" was not a word he'd apply to himself.

That changed now. Though he wasn't sure how.

Especially not when both sides were watching with such suspicion, especially her people.

Marrok sucked in a breath, straightening. "I'll meet you at the car. Don't go before I get there."

He turned to find her watching him with a posture that screamed wariness. "You're not going to fight me on this?" she asked.

Of course he was, but he needed more than just words right now.

"Promise me?"

After a brief hesitation, she nodded. "You have my word."

Thank the gods for small mercies. Marrok turned and left the room. Determination straightened his spine as he hurried to put his plan into action. He *would* fix this.

He'd make sure they could lead together…or he'd give up his position as alpha.

. . .

I'm doing the right thing.

Her new mantra. Maybe if she repeated it enough times in her head, she'd believe it. He hadn't been wrong about their physical connection growing, not that she'd tell him that. But her intense attraction to Marrok was dangerous so long as the imbalance in their alpha roles remained. They needed to stay apart until they figured that out.

Tala exited the foyer already knowing her mate stood outside waiting beside her sister. His scent reached her in the elevator.

Tala did her best not to twitch uncomfortably at the light in his eyes. The truth was, she was still pissed at him. She'd been pissed last night, too, but the second they touched, her body had taken over. Hell, even right now, if he touched her, she'd probably melt into a puddle at the damn man's feet. This need for him was a complication she hadn't counted on.

Her wolf tried to ignore how incredible he smelled—woodsy, earthy. Alpha. He gave off such an air of confidence, she couldn't help but respond to it. At the same time, Tala's heart twisted inside her, as though he'd reached into her chest and crushed it in those big hands that had been instruments of pleasure since the moment of their mating.

He was letting her go.

Irritation followed on the disappointment, like sandpaper to her skin. This was what she wanted. Hadn't she been telling him to listen to her? She couldn't get upset about him finally doing just that.

Or was this what he'd wanted all along? Her out of the way.

With a huff, her wolf turned away and lay down in her head. Her animal was still angry, too, apparently.

No that wasn't it.

Tala had observed her wolf's reactions closely since trying to take a hunk out of Marrok—her animal side was attracted to their mate, respected him, but resented him, too. Enough that she couldn't be trusted around him. Why? Because he was too alpha for her?

No. As far as Tala could tell, her wolf viewed Marrok, in both his forms, as her equal. Perhaps that was it? No other alpha could claim equal status until now, and her wolf took that as a threat? That didn't feel like it, either. Whatever drove her animal, a dark emotion swirled inside her.

One more fucking complication.

Before Tala could pinpoint the issue, another car pulled up behind Astra's. The driver, one of Marrok's men, got out and handed him the car keys before leaving.

Slowly, she made her way down the wide steps to both of them. A quick glance at her sister showed her watching with quiet interest. Unusual for her. Did she sense the same determination from Marrok that Tala was feeling?

Ignoring Astra for the moment, Tala stopped before her mate.

"Can I run an idea past you before you decide to leave?" he asked. Softly.

He was asking, not telling. That alone had her wolf pricking her ears. Curiosity piqued despite her determination to remain distant. She crossed her arms against the pull he had for her. "What is it?"

His mouth tightened almost imperceptibly. "I propose you and I go somewhere. Alone."

She drew her brows down, even as her heart gave an extra thump. "What for?"

He searched her eyes, but she gave him nothing.

"You've said I have to share being alpha, and I have to earn you…"

Her heart rate wanted to speed up, but with effort she forced it to remain steady and gave a small nod for him to continue.

"I want to do that. I want to make this work. For our packs…and for us."

Did he really mean this? She remained silent, waiting.

"It seems to me," he continued, "the best way is to spend time alone, without our packs watching and the pressures of leading. If we got to know each other better—" He waved a hand.

Tala tried not to find the fact endearing that he was floundering with what had to be a new situation. "You want to take a honeymoon?"

His amazing blue eyes flared with desire, only to be banked to smoldering. Tala swallowed.

"No sex," Marrok said.

Okay... Her wolf cocked her head. "No sex," Tala said slowly.

"Correct. In addition to getting to know each other better, we'd spend time hammering out details for our packs and how we want to lead. Together. Then, when we return to our packs, we'll be on the same page."

She had to admit his plan had merit. More important, he wasn't issuing a demand. That alone was a step in the right direction. *Can we keep our hands off each other, though?* Even now her body strained toward him; she wanted his hands on her body, him inside her, over her, around her...

Marrok interrupted her contemplation. "I think we can, if we both agree. Alphas have more willpower than most."

Tala blinked, and her face flared hot. Had she said that aloud? Or had he sensed it through their link? What she got from him was minimal. A flash here and there. "How long are you thinking?" she asked.

"A week to start. More or less depending on the progress we make."

Now he was making this sound like a business deal only. Irritation lanced through her. At herself. Their marriage *was* a business deal only. She had no right or reason to wish for... more.

"Where?"

"The cabin."

Her cabin?

They hadn't talked about it since the days right after their mating and her bid to help the nymph who'd risked so much for them. Marrok wanted to go *there*?

"There's only one bed in there." She chanced a glance at Astra who, thankfully, continued to watch all this in silence.

"I'll sleep on the couch," Marrok said.

She would *not* be disappointed. She'd told him he had to earn his way back into her bed, and she meant it. Tala pursed her lips. "Okay."

"Okay?" Again, he searched her expression, eyes intent. "As in yes?"

"I agree with your plan."

When it came down to it, deciding to leave him was the hardest damn thing she'd ever had to do. That, in and of itself, was a shock to her system. Jarring. Like walking into a glass door when you thought nothing was there.

Usually a master at hiding her emotions, she honestly had no idea what she was feeling, and, therefore, what he was seeing. Or what he felt about her agreement. He was equally proficient at concealing his emotions. She focused on that elusive connection, more faint today than it had been the night they mated. An echo reached to her, like her own footsteps inside a tunnel. Satisfaction seemed to be a big part of his reaction. Satisfaction and…relief. Relief? That emotion would indicate an emotional investment in this working.

Of course, he's invested, dummy. His pack needs the peace as much as yours.

Marrok touched her hand softly. "I want this to work for us as much as for our people."

Seriously. Was the man a mind reader?

Abruptly he turned away and started moving her luggage from Astra's car to his own, which already had his own suitcase in the trunk.

Tala moved to give her sister a hug. "You're still in charge while I'm gone."

"I figured. Good luck," Astra whispered in her ear, then got in her car and drove away.

Marrok stood at the driver's side door waiting, and Tala moved around to the passenger side slowly, running her mind over his actions and words and what she'd just agreed to.

A small beacon of hope sparked inside her. Maybe this mating could work after all. The cautious voice in her head—not that of her wolf, who was anything but cautious and still wary—but her own self, warned her to reserve judgment.

She'd give Marrok a week. Then they'd see.

Chapter Eight

The cabin, so familiar, was tucked away in the middle of the wilderness. Tala had been born in this cabin, long before being an alpha was even an inkling of a thought to her family.

The building was as basic as you could get, smelling of the pine trees from which the logs had been hewn. It boasted a combined kitchen and living area with a small separate bathroom on the first floor and a ladder leading up to a loft that functioned as a bedroom. Minimal furniture, a power generator, and a well system for water afforded all the required comforts of living. A large pond was situated within walking distance, down a steep hill from the flat clearing on which the cabin was situated.

The winding route to get here had taken a good few hours. After enjoying a private run around the property, letting her wolf out to roam, at Marrok's suggestion, she felt worlds better. Looser. Freer here, away from all those judging gazes.

After shifting, she swiftly pulled on a pair of jeans and navy cotton tank top. She wrapped a thick leather belt around her waist and twisted her hair up, securing it with her hair sticks. Finally, she pulled on a pair of hiking boots Leia had left behind and tied them up. Then let herself into the cabin.

"What's this?" Tala couldn't contain her shocked outburst at finding Marrok in the kitchen.

Alpha males did *not* cook. Period.

Hell, she was an alpha female, and she didn't cook. Nevertheless, the cabin was filled with the mouthwatering scent of ground beef, and a pot of water boiled softly on the cooktop. Her stomach chose that instant to gurgle, and her wolf lolled her tongue at the prospect of food. Dang, she was famished.

A good run always did that to her.

Her mate turned and grinned over his shoulder, his eyes crinkling in a playful way that tugged at her heart.

"Spaghetti." He waved at a jar of sauce on the counter with his spatula. "Nothing fancy."

Why did a simple act like cooking dinner for her make her feel all warm and fuzzy? Tala wasn't sure she wanted to inspect the emotion further. Weakness in an alpha wasn't going to get her anywhere. And Marrok could be a big weakness.

"Can I help?" Doing something, anything, would make this uncomfortable, stomach- churning sensation go away.

"You can sit and take a break."

Tala eyed the small wood table with two chairs as if it were a snake that might bite her.

"Problem?"

"I don't sit still well," she murmured. She was almost as bad as a hummingbird shifter that way.

Marrok's deep laugh pulled her out of her head. She hadn't meant to say that out loud. The rumbling sound warmed her from the inside out. She'd always liked his laugh, from the very first moment. Wouldn't mind hearing it more.

Her shoulders slumped. She wasn't funny or witty, so getting him to laugh with her was about as likely as making the change without pain. Irritation followed closely on the heels of her uncharacteristic self-pity. What was she thinking?

To distract herself, she set the table and got them both water. Enjoying the blast of cool against her skin, she got the ice out of trays from the freezer, popping each cube out with a satisfying push.

Then she pulled together a basic salad from the few fresh veggies in the fridge. She searched the cabinets. "Only olive oil for dressing I'm afraid."

"That's fine."

Out of things to do, she finally sat. With nothing else to focus on, she watched her mate as he shuffled around the small space. His movements smooth and easy, he obviously was comfortable in a kitchen. Damn, did he have a fantastic ass. Memories of digging her claws into him, kneading him, assailed her, turning up her core temperature more than a few notches. She forced her gaze away, focusing instead on the familiar view outside the window.

Thankfully, he put a plate down in front of her only a few minutes later. A soft moan escaped her as the first tangy bite hit her tongue. Hungry didn't begin to describe the yawning pit in her stomach. "This is good."

"Thanks."

A tension in his voice fairly crackled through the tenuous mating connection and had her glancing up to find him staring at her lips with utter fascination. An answering heat flared and fused with her blood, moving through her body, but Marrok dragged his gaze away, breaking the intimacy. Their connection went dark, as though he'd turned off whatever he was feeling.

Just like she did.

They spent the first few minutes concentrating on eating.

The change always made her ravenous.

"So…"

She glanced up at Marrok's hesitation to find him watching her with interest. She raised her eyebrows in question.

"Tell me about your family," he prompted.

Now she dropped her brows in a frown as she finished chewing a bite. "Why?"

"Other than Astra, they weren't at the mating ceremony. Are they still alive?"

She shook her head. "My parents died about five years ago. Car crash." One the pack had blamed on the Banes clan but Tala secretly suspected had come from within her own. She'd been rising quickly in the ranks at the time.

He reached across and gave her hand a squeeze. "I'm sorry."

That he truly meant it gave her an odd warm fuzzy sensation again. His hand against hers was also warm…and strong and managed to send sizzles of sensation through her. At a simple touch. Gods, she was turning into a wimp with him.

"Were you close?" he asked.

She dropped her gaze and twirled a noodle on her fork. "Yes. They were devoted to each other. Both submissives, they were childhood sweethearts."

"Rare for submissives to give birth to an alpha."

"Two. Astra's an alpha, too."

He grinned. "No interest in leading, I take it."

She pursed her lips. "None. Though she's stepped up lately, with me on Banes land."

"But you wanted to be alpha?" The question was one she was used to.

She shrugged. "My parents were idealists. They raised me to believe all the bloodshed was preventable. They believed a woman alpha would bring reason to the role, which could end the fighting, saving lives on both sides."

"So they encouraged you to become alpha?"

"Not entirely. Their idea of a woman alpha was more theoretical. But I'm...driven, and I agreed with them. If I could end the fighting, that would be worth everything it took to become alpha." As well as everything she sacrificed personally. Uncomfortable talking about herself this much, she tilted her head, curiosity getting the better of her. "What about you?"

"I was raised not far from where we were mated until I was ten, at which point I moved to the pack community housing. My father was alpha before me, as you probably know."

She nodded around a sip of water. Everyone in the wolf shifter community knew of Channon Banes.

"He wanted me to start life without the pressure and recognition of being the alpha's son."

"Who did you live with?"

"My grandparents."

"That must've been hard for your mother."

"Maternal is not a word I'd use for her, but my grandparents were wonderful people. They disagreed with the fighting, which is why they lived away from the pack."

That explained much of his willingness to seek peace, if he'd been raised believing the fighting to be wrong.

"As you also know, your previous alpha killed my father."

She froze with her fork halfway to her mouth. Slowly she lowered it. "His death is why I challenged for alpha when I did."

Marrok leaned back in his chair, eyeing her thoughtfully. "Why?"

"Your father's death wasn't warranted or right. He'd come to negotiate a truce. Eyolf killed him in cold blood."

"So you challenged him."

He left unsaid the fact that if Eyolf had been strong enough to take down his father, an intimidating wolf shifter with a reputation, then Tala's abilities were perhaps greater than expected. She caught the realization in his eyes, nonetheless.

Marrok blew out a long breath and ran his hands through his hair, mussing the dark waves in an adorably haphazard fashion. "Thank you for that."

She glanced away and shrugged one shoulder. "It was the right thing to do. Eyolf made many bad decisions for my pack." Time to change the subject. "Is your mother still alive?"

"Yes." The tightening around his mouth told her a tension existed between mother and son. "She's visiting an old friend in the Pyrenees."

Right. "Not happy about you mating your enemy?" she guessed.

"She'll come around when we have her first grandchild."

Tala startled, shock zipping across her nerve endings, stiffening her spine. Children. She honestly hadn't thought that far ahead. Keeping their packs from killing one another and dealing with their mating was enough to keep her brain fully occupied.

The mental image of carrying Marrok's child in her belly, looking forward to the birth of that child, sent butterflies fluttering through her insides. Nice ones. Shock splintered through her at the realization. She *wanted* a child. Not any child. Marrok's.

But could they get past this alpha issue?

She did her best to hide her astonishment as they finished dinner. Marrok was a surprisingly good listener. Under his gentle questioning, Tala found herself opening up to him as they talked about nothing in particular but still learned about each other. After dinner, Tala insisted on doing the dishes, since he'd cooked. They chatted more while she washed the dishes, then naturally migrated to the love seat in the small living area. Before she knew it, night had fallen.

After Tala yawned for the fifth or sixth time, Marrok laughed. He stood and pulled her to her feet. "Time for bed, sleepyhead."

Warmth flushed through her in the most pleasant, surprising way, and an answering desire danced in his eyes. Instead of pulling her into his arms, though, he stepped back.

Her confusion must've shown on her face, because he reached out and brushed her cheek. "I won't come to your bed until you trust me."

Her eyes widened as disappointment warred with pride.

"You told me I had to earn my way into your heart, and I mean to."

Actually, she'd said bed, but okay. For now, she couldn't let that small slip be a distraction. This time apart was about their packs and leadership first and foremost.

"I see." She inhaled, gathering the strength to move away from him. With effort she did manage it, stepping back and over to the ladder leading to the loft, where the only bed was located. She glanced over her shoulder to find he hadn't moved. "Goodnight."

"Sweet dreams...mate."

• • •

Tala's nose twitched as the rich aroma of coffee wafted to where she slept in the loft. She groaned as she rolled over and stretched. Sleep had eluded her last night as she'd lain in bed with her incredibly sexy, frustrating mate downstairs on the floor. The small love seat had not been big enough to hold his bulk, but even sleeping stretched out on the floor he seemed uncomfortable, and, as fully awake as she was, Tala could hear him moving around.

A thousand times she'd debated going to him, answering the clamoring needs of her body. Even more so the strangest need to just be near him.

But, in the end, she hadn't.

She'd meant it when she said he had to earn his way into her bed. This mission he was on now, caring for her, giving them time to discuss and agree on actions alone in order to present a united front to their people, was a good start. Before she rushed into trusting him, though, she needed to see him carry it through when they had an audience.

Could he be both alpha and mate, not letting one get in the way of the other? Could she?

Sunlight poured through the triangular window directly across from the loft. Another gorgeous day in the mountains. Her wolf perked up. Maybe later today she could take a run.

The need for caffeine had her throwing back the covers. She pulled a sweater over her pajama bottoms and tank top and climbed downstairs on silent, bare feet.

"Morning," Marrok rumbled as she stepped off the bottom rung of the ladder.

Damn, the man had a sexy morning voice, all gravelly and low, the sound skittering up and down her spine in a delicious way. That, combined with the fact that he wore only boxer briefs, the band sitting just low enough that the ridge of muscle arrowing downward was on stark display for her greedy eyes, was enough to make any woman drool.

She cleared her throat and ignored the sweet ache now lingering. "Morning."

He stood at the stove cooking again—scrambled eggs.

Good mate. Tala pointed out to her wolf.

The fickle creature huffed, unimpressed.

Tala scooted around him, tempted to "accidentally" brush up against that fabulous ass, grabbed a mug on the counter she assumed he'd gotten out for her, filled it, then stirred in buckets of cream and sugar. She dropped into a chair at the table, pulling one leg in close, her foot propped on her seat, knee up by her chest, and took a long, grateful swig.

"So you take coffee with your cream and sugar?" Laughter lurked in his voice, and she glanced over the rim of her mug to find him watching her, lips quirked.

She put her mug down and grinned. "It's basically dessert. I can't drink it too often or I'll get chubby." She pulled a face.

"Somehow I doubt that." He eyed her slender form, appreciation sparking in those electric blue eyes.

How he managed to touch her without physically coming near her was a mystery, but Tala's body was on fire, nonetheless. She shifted in her seat, trying to ease the need, so tempted to scratch the itch instead of resist. "What's on the agenda today?"

He turned back to the eggs, lifting the pan off the stove and turning off the burner. "Breakfast. Then discussion. I'd like you to make a list of the issues you want to hit first. I thought we'd cover those, then, if there's anything else on my list, we'll hit them afterward."

Sounded reasonable. "Okay."

Already her mind was ticking over the countless items on her side. Everything from living arrangements, to feeding both packs, to sharing of assets, to dealing with multiple people in the same positions—two alphas, two seconds-in-command, two sets of councillors, various enforcers, and so forth. Combining their packs was like combining two fully functioning corporations or townships with all the complications each entailed.

And the added fun of mutual, senseless hate. Don't forget that part.

Marrok set her plate down in front of her and took his

own seat. On autopilot Tala took a bite and had to stuff down a groan. Spaghetti and scrambled eggs, the two meals he'd made, weren't exactly cordon bleu, but the man could cook. "These are fantastic."

"They're just eggs." Eyebrows lifted, he eyed her curiously.

She scrunched up her nose. "I live on power bars mostly."

Something he'd know if they had any time to themselves. Instead they always seemed to be rushing from meeting to meeting, putting out fires, grabbing what they could to eat along the way.

"Ah." He took a bite of his eggs.

That was it? "I can't cook. I don't clean. I've never changed a diaper in my life. I don't do soft and cuddly. I'm ultra-competitive. And sentiment makes me…uncomfortable."

He paused mid-chew and cocked his head, searching her expression. Then he swallowed the bite. "Why are you telling me all this?"

"You need to know what you're getting with me." She glanced outside the window over the sink. "Maybe I'm not the mate you need." The last she murmured softly.

"Hey." Marrok leaned across the table and took her chin in his fingers, forcing her gaze back to him. "You're exactly the mate I need."

The conviction in his words, in his eyes, chipped away at the cold block of ice and fear surrounding her heart.

Marrok released her, letting her breathe more easily as he leaned back in his chair. "I can cook; in fact, I like it. I don't clean, either, but pay one of the ladies from the pack to come in for me, though I'm neat. I've never changed a diaper, either, but when babies come, we'll figure it out together. I suspect I'm more of a cuddler than you, but you've been cuddly enough for me so far."

The heat turning his eyes even more blue brought warmth

to her cheeks. "I'm also ultra-competitive, which should make for an interesting life together." He grinned now. "But I don't give up, either, and no matter how mad you get at me, this mating is for life. While I'm not sentimental in general, I have a feeling you may change that for me, so you'll just have to deal with it when I get mushy on you."

"Oh." Tala bit her lip as another piece of ice fell away. He'd managed to get to the heart of every one of her fears. At the core of Marrok Banes existed a solid, decent man. Someone she genuinely liked, which was rare for her. Maybe he did see her, the real her, and didn't appear intimidated… or put off.

Maybe they could do this.

Time to see how he negotiated. She sat forward in her chair and picked up her fork. "What are your thoughts on choosing a new neutral site to reestablish both packs together?"

Chapter Nine

Marrok's gaze followed his mate as she paced back and forth in front of the stone fireplace. Damn, she was amazing. But everything she'd wanted to talk about had to do with the packs and running them together.

At least they'd decided on what seemed like a reasonable splitting of alpha duties, outlining different roles that only one of them would take on. Tala would be in charge of defense, education, social needs, and dealing with humans. Marrok had agreed to take on training of their fighters, living quarters, settlement development, and dealing with outside supernatural groups like the Alliance of dragon shifters and the Covens Syndicate of witches. They'd also agreed on areas that they both had to be in on the decisions and discussions.

This was good, if frustrating, progress.

Three days. Three days of nonstop discussions about the packs while resisting touching her, reaching for her, and sleeping on the fucking couch, got worse with every passing day.

His cock might petrify, it had been hard for so long.

It didn't help that Tala showed him her more casual side, discarding her usual fancier suits and dresses.

They'd both opted for jeans each day, including today. While he'd pulled on another black T-shirt, his go-to casual wear, she'd gone with a white tank top with glittery stuff highlighting her lovely breasts. He particularly liked how the soft jeans she'd donned hugged her tight backside. Oh, to be those jeans.

Trying to be stealthy about it, Marrok shifted in his seat for the umpteenth time, in a useless attempt to relieve the pulsing pressure in his crotch.

Their scents—his earthy and hers with a hint of wildflowers—mingled in the small space. They'd both foregone shoes, and their bare feet gave the impression of intimacy. Or maybe he was entertaining wishful thinking? They'd been talking today already through the morning, through lunch, and now through part of the afternoon.

And not one word about the "them" part of coming together as alphas beyond the logistics of it. The pack came first, as it should. Was that all she was interested in saving?

Protect our mate, his wolf pushed at him.

Protect? But she wasn't in danger. At least, not right now, and he doubted she'd appreciate that kind of effort.

Protect, his wolf urged.

Did he mean care for? His wolf nosed at him.

Take care of his mate. The idea settled in Marrok's heart. Tala was independent, strong, tough. Had she ever let anyone take care of her? Would she let him? Worth a shot if it meant winning her. But he'd have to be subtle in the way he went about it. She'd already shown a disdain for overt signs of caring.

"We need a set of laws concerning the mixing of the packs, or they're likely to kill one another." She flung her hands up in frustration.

"I agree."

"You don't—" She stopped and swung toward him. "You agree?"

That she'd expected him to argue was clearly a mark against them both. "Yes. Until we all view each individual as family, as pack, rather than as 'us versus them,' or as enemies, it won't work."

"Exactly."

"I also think it's time we take a break." He glanced at his watch pointedly.

Tala peeked at the slim band on her own wrist and grimaced. "We have been going at this a long time."

He set down his laptop, which he'd been using to take notes, and held out his hand. "Come on."

Tentatively, she placed her hand in his. "Where are we going?"

"For a run?" he suggested. His wolf was begging him to get out and stretch his legs, explore this area, play with his mate. Maybe. The animal yipped excitedly in his head. Marrok was less sure that could happen.

Tala pulled back at that, but he tightened his grip, keeping her close.

"I could kill you," she said. "My wolf—"

"Was pissed about me stepping all over your alpha-ness. Right?"

"Maybe," she said slowly.

Through the tentative connection binding them as mates he sensed the give in her, though her body remained tense.

"Let's do this… I'll shift first. Then face me as you shift. Last time, she seemed surprised I was there. If you go at me, I'll be ready."

Tala's gaze slid away from his.

"We need to be able to shift together," he insisted. "Do you want to figure it out here, where no one else can witness it? Or back with our packs."

Tala sighed. "Here."

Good. "I'll go first."

After her nod, he proceeded to shift. Tala held herself still as he moved through the process slower than normal, not wanting to pose any threat to her. He'd been told his black coloring gave him a more sinister appearance. He also stood several inches taller than most male wolf shifters, broader in the shoulders. Not as big as their werewolf ancestors, who were twice his size, but still, intimidating.

Shift complete, his wolf took over for a second, approaching his mate cautiously until he stood directly in front of her. Then loosed a small whining sound which made her eyebrows go up.

"I'm okay," she said softly.

He butted her hand with his nose, then proceeded to rub against her. Tala gave a low chuckle before giving in and running her fingers through his thick fur, gaining a rumble of satisfaction from the wolf before Marrok regained control.

As much as he wanted to enjoy her touch, they needed to do this. Backing up, he gave her space to make her shift without feeling threatened. Deliberately he stood beside the open door to the cabin.

Gaze trained on his, Tala took a long breath, then called her wolf forward, ceding control to the animal, though not completely, he knew. If she could hold that edge where her human side was in charge even as the animal was freed, maybe she wouldn't attack. A delicate balance of give and take. Her body shimmered and shifted until the white wolf stood before him.

"Tala?" he called out softly. Could she hear him this time?

She blinked for a moment as though reorienting herself, then, with no warning, lunged for him.

Plan already in place, Marrok leaped for the open door, got around it, and put a shoulder to the back side, slamming it shut a heartbeat before something hard and heavy bashed into it. Tala, based on the snarls ripping from the wolf's throat on the other side of the door.

Practically feral, no amount of trying to get her to talk to him helped.

Marrok gave up and shifted, defeat gripping him so hard his heart ached, then he waited her out, sitting with his back to the door, arms draped over his knees.

Fuck.

Her wolf wanted to kill him still. Why? They'd been doing better. *He'd* been doing better.

Quiet eventually descended outside, even the birds in the trees going silent. "I'm okay now," Tala called through the door.

Standing, Marrok swung the door open to find her there, pale, with an apology in her eyes, reaching down that connection to him. A connection he hadn't felt with her wolf.

And different. He couldn't put his finger on different how. But something in her had changed, he could feel it.

Tala let loose a low sigh. "Maybe we're trying to force something that will never work."

No. Panic clawed at his insides. She couldn't give up on him, on them. He stepped across the threshold and took her face in his hands and waited until she looked at him. "Don't ever say that—"

The shrill ring of a phone interrupted him. *Shit. What now?*

"I'll get it." Tala moved around him to the kitchen.

"Hello?" she answered as she dropped heavily into one of the wooden chairs. She paused and listened, suddenly intent. "Damn," she muttered. "Send a car. I'll be waiting."

She hung up and turned to Marrok. "I've been challenged for alpha formally. I have to go."

Chapter Ten

Marrok placed his hands on the roof and door of the SUV and leaned inside to stare at his mate, who stared back with a frustratingly calm expression. Calm? Hell, she was blank. Not a single emotion. The mating connection was a dead line, not even static reaching him. Meanwhile, his wolf raged inside him.

"You're really going to do this alone? I should be there. At your side."

She shook her head. "I need to show them I'm still alpha. Without you."

Bile rose in his throat, sour in his mouth. He got the logic of her decision, but the thought of not being there when she could die gutted him, went against every protective instinct he had as her mate.

Letting her go was the hardest thing he'd ever done, a physical pain inside him, razor blades against his skin. Every cell screamed at him to go with her. His wolf clawed at his insides, trying to force him to do something. Go with her.

"I'll stay away tonight," he agreed, his voice gone hoarse

with his wolf so close to the surface. "But I'm coming tomorrow. No matter what."

A tiny smile pulled at her lips, and she gave a quick nod. His panic didn't ease, but at least she hadn't said no. She wanted him with her. He'd take that as progress.

"You're not allowed to die on me."

"I'm not planning to."

"Swear it," he pressed. "By the moon."

The air within the car stilled as Tala lifted her gaze to his, searching. For what? "Not by the moon," she said softly. "The moon is inconstant, ever changing."

Marrok huffed a laugh tinged in bitter reality. "Not unlike a woman."

She would not swear, he could see it in her eyes. Unable to not touch her any longer—these were special circumstances, dammit—Marrok leaned in and kissed her. Their lips clung, lingered, and the fire of need blazed in him at the sweet taste of her, the way she sighed into him, opened for him.

Tala pulled back first. She kept her eyes closed and breathed deeply. Her heart rate even picked up a fraction. *Good.* He wasn't the only one affected.

"I'll see you tomorrow," he promised. The plan was for her to return to him here after she was done.

She opened those amazing green eyes and he almost took it back as she allowed him to witness her fear and worry, like the shadow of the moon over her features. "Tomorrow," she said.

Marrok stepped back and shut the door. He tapped the roof with the flat of his hand and the driver hit the gas. The SUV bumped away on the rudimentary dirt track.

Marrok's wolf gave a howl of mixed fury and terror for his mate. Marrok didn't feel any better about watching her drive away. Tala was right. This was her fight. But instinct was a bitch, and every cell in his body screamed that he should be with her.

. . .

Tala refused to look back to see if Marrok watched as she drove away. If she did, she might turn around and run straight back into his arms.

A few basic meals, some decent discussion, and I almost take his wolf out. Now being away from him made it harder to breathe, unforgiving bands trapping her lungs.

With sheer force of will, she pushed the sensation down and instead opened her laptop to pull up the reports Astra had sent. Running a pack was like being mayor of a small town or CEO of a medium business. The job came with all the same headaches and complications. Basic services like electricity, water, trash. People management, including employment, health care, regulation. Financial needs were huge. Although their communities were essentially self-contained, they still had to function in the wider world or they would draw human attention. There were also the special needs of wolf shifters—keeping new wolves from attacking humans, intra-pack issues, inter-pack issues.

Feuds.

The lists went on and on, and she'd neglected those duties these past few days hidden away with Marrok.

Dwelling on the challenge she faced was a waste of effort, so Tala tried to lose herself in the reports, making notes of things she needed to check on or investigate further, meetings to set up, and other needs. She glanced up briefly when the ride abruptly shifted from bumpy to smooth as they hit asphalt road about an hour from the cabin. Another hour later, she glanced up again.

She twisted in her seat, taking a closer look at their surroundings. This area wasn't remotely familiar. "Dolph?"

she called to the driver. "Where are we?"

"Road closures meant we had to reroute."

His words made sense, but something in his tone snagged her attention. As she listened, his heart rate increased.

"I see." She deliberately relaxed into her seat and pretended to go back to her work, and his heart rate reverted to normal.

Something was definitely off here. Usually not prone to being easily alarmed, the warning sirens going off in her head had Tala acting on instinct. She slipped her phone from her backpack. Keeping it out of Dolph's line of sight, she dialed the number Marrok had given her. She couldn't risk putting it on speaker or Dolph would hear her mate. With his enhanced hearing, he might hear, anyway, but she had to take that risk.

"Do you mind if we stop?"

He glanced at her in the rearview mirror. "Why?"

She waved at her computer. "Reading on a bumpy road was a terrible idea. I'm not feeling well."

He shook his head. "We're not far from the town of Rand."

The exact opposite direction from where they'd been headed and dragon shifter territory. "Rand?" She played it cool. "Wow. We really did get rerouted."

Dolph grunted in agreement.

"I assume we got permission from the Alliance to be here?"

Another grunt that she supposed could be an affirmative. But doubted it.

She pushed the button for the window, but it refused to budge. "Can you unlock the window?"

"Why?"

In the rearview mirror, Tala pinned him with her iciest stare. "Because I want to roll it down. Fresh air might help."

Dolph remained silent.

Tala's wolf started to pace. Very slowly she tightened her

seatbelt. "Stop the car."

No response.

Tala imbued the command with all the alpha at her disposal. "I said—"

Dolph pulled out a pistol and aimed it straight at her.

In a flash Tala threw her computer at him. The heavy projectile struck him in the head. Reflex made him squeeze the trigger, and the gun went off. Dolph slumped forward, out cold, and the SUV swerved as his heavy body turned the wheel. Tala braced herself as the vehicle slammed into the granite rock of the mountain, the impact jarring, throwing her against her seatbelt so hard, pain spiked through her right side and her head snapped back and forth. The world upended as they flipped onto the roof and skidded, with a sickening screech of metal on asphalt, before slamming to an abrupt halt that jolted her so hard, she felt like a ragdoll being shaken by a dog.

Dazed, she took a second to breathe and evaluate her situation. Nothing more than bumps and bruises, maybe a cracked rib, thank the gods. The distinct, tinny scent of gasoline filled the air. The fumes also served to clear her head. Time to move. With a *click*, she released her seatbelt and dropped to her hands and knees, ignoring the bite of glass in her palms. The doors were locked and wouldn't unlock from the backseat.

She grabbed her phone, which lay among the rubble, and scrambled between the seats up to the front. She managed to maneuver around Dolph's unconscious form, giving a grim smile at the sight of blood oozing from a cut on the back of his head, and hit the button to unlock the doors, but the passenger door wouldn't budge when she went to open it. Tala closed her eyes and accessed the full strength of her wolf. With a mighty shove and the wail of metal against metal, she forced the door open, barely wide enough for her to squeeze out.

She held up her cell phone and swore at the spider web pattern on the screen. Sure enough, when she went to turn it on, the display was all scrambled. Dolph was unconscious but could wake any moment. Who knew how close or far his fellow traitors were from her? Tala was convinced Dolph had been taking her to others, likely to kill her.

She needed to move. Now.

Tala hustled up into the trees on the other side of the road. She closed her eyes and breathed deeply before willing the change. Only a whimper escaped her lips as her body accommodated its four-legged form, injuries from the crash adding a slice of pain.

Time for brains over brawn. She took off through the forest. Hopefully, the damn dragons weren't anywhere close. They didn't exactly love wolf shifters. Especially an alpha.

Chapter Eleven

After Tala had driven away, Marrok hadn't been able to sit still. He had a few more hours before his own ride arrived. While he might not be able to stay with his mate in her territory, he could at least be close by. While he waited, he decided a run as a wolf would help bleed off this sense of wrongness inside him.

Wolf shifters found nature soothing, and he needed soothing.

After shifting quickly, he took off into the surrounding woods. He ran and ran. No purpose, no direction guided his paws. With all his heart, he wished Tala was at his side, gorgeous with her white and gray coat and smooth movements.

Had their few days together been enough?

Eventually Marrok knew he had to go back. For a brief moment, he tilted his face to the sky and enjoyed the breeze ruffling his fur. He dug his claws into the hard ground and enjoyed the power of his muscles tightly coiled. But the need for his mate turned his feet toward the cabin.

As he neared the clearing, his pace slowed to an easy

lope, then a trot. A truck built for off-road, with large tires and roll bar, stood parked out front. Marrok circled the clearing, still hidden in the woods, and cautiously sniffed the air. Recognizing the scent of one of his people, he relaxed and emerged.

Outside the cabin he took the minute to make the change, then stepped inside to find Rafe waiting for him at the small kitchen table.

"I won't take long," Marrok said.

The other wolf shifter, never much of a talker, gave him a thumbs-up.

Marrok pulled on his jeans and had his T-shirt over his head when his phone rang. He yanked the shirt down and grabbed the device off the coffee table. Tala's number popped up on the display, and he answered. "Tala?"

A short silence greeted him, but he could hear the noise of her SUV on the road. "Tala?" he repeated.

"Do you mind if we stop?" Her voice was faint, far away from the phone.

Panic slammed through him so hard he had to slap both hands on the table to keep from collapsing. Stop what? She wanted to stop their mating? Stop the truce? What? He thought they'd made progress. "Baby, wait—"

"Why?" A male voice cut him off. He recognized Dolph, the Canis shifter who'd picked her up. Marrok frowned and listened.

Tala spoke next. "Reading on a bumpy road was a terrible idea. I'm not feeling well." Had she butt-dialed him?

"We're not far from the town of Rand."

Marrok cocked his head. Rand was the exact opposite direction from where Tala was going. Also, dragon shifter territory. "Rand," she said, still sounding perfectly calm. "Wow. We really did get rerouted."

Dolph grunted in agreement.

"I assume we got permission from the Alliance to be here?"

Another grunted response.

Another pause. "Can you unlock the window?" Tala asked next.

Something was definitely wrong. This was too casual. Too coincidental. No way had she dialed him by accident. Not only did he seriously doubt Tala ever got carsick, but she was nervous. Marrok could hear it in her voice, though he doubted Dolph could. Marrok knew his mate. How he did after a relatively short time with her was beyond him. Perhaps their bond was strengthening. Regardless, her nerves jangled across the line at him.

"Why?" Dolph asked.

"Because I want to roll it down." No irritation laced her words. "Fresh air might help."

Dolph remained silent.

"Stop the car." She'd changed from requesting to ordering.

No response.

"I said—"

A soft gasp reached his ears. If he hadn't been a wolf shifter, he wouldn't have caught it. The unmistakable pop of gunfire was followed by what sounded like the racket of a car crash. Panic slammed through Marrok again, his heart taking off like a sprinter, adrenaline scorching his veins, and his wolf pushed to be released.

Marrok gripped the phone. "Tala?" he yelled.

No answer.

"Tala!"

But the line was dead.

Marrok breathed hard. He had to think, had to save his mate. His wolf was frantic inside his head.

"Boss?" Rafe's snarl caught Marrok's attention, and he

raised his head to find the wolf shifter beside him.

"Did you hear all that?"

A nod.

Marrok shoved the phone at him. "Keys."

Rafe fished them out and put them in Marrok's outstretched hand before he followed Marrok out to the truck.

"Call Astra first," Marrok ordered as they got in. Tala's sister might be in danger, too. "Then call Blaez." Rafe would understand Marrok meant to have the commander of their fighters rally the troops.

He cranked the engine and took off through the trees. White-knuckled, he gripped the wheel, pushing the truck over the rough terrain faster than was prudent. How long had he been out there running? If they were close to Rand, they were almost two hours away.

He had to get to Tala.

· · ·

Ninety minutes later, Marrok crouched beside the demolished SUV his mate had driven away in this morning. Only iron will and the knowledge that losing his shit wouldn't help had him biting knife-edged fury slashing through him. Fury because otherwise he'd be in a dead panic. His wolf clawed at his insides, slamming against his skin in a frenzy to get out. He'd loose the beast soon enough, but first he needed to determine a plan.

The vehicle had been abandoned. A small pool of blood stained the ground on the driver's side. Marrok trailed his fingers through it and inhaled. Not Tala. The scent of her blood was sweeter, richer. He'd tasted it when he'd claimed her. This blood was sharper, almost darker. Dolph probably. *Good.* He hoped that fucker was bleeding to death somewhere in the woods.

"Boss," Rafe called from the tree line.

Marrok rose and crossed to where he stood.

"Look." Rafe indicated a series of paw prints. The smaller set had to be Tala. He could smell her—earth and wildflowers, like the field at their cabin. His wolf snarled. More prints followed hers into the woods. Tala was being hunted.

These prints were larger and deeper, male wolf shifters—at least six of them. Too many for Tala to fight on her own. The new set of prints were fresher, the scents stronger, more recent. At a guess, he was only twenty minutes behind them, which meant Tala had a decent head start, assuming she wasn't hampered by injury and Dolph hadn't gotten to her already.

Marrok yanked his shirt over his head. "I'm going after her. Stay here and wait for the others."

Rafe opened his mouth to argue, but shut it, his jaw squared, and nodded.

"I'll leave an obvious trail to follow." He didn't wait for Rafe to acknowledge. The change couldn't come fast enough. He willed his body to adjust and reform faster. His wolf practically burst from his skin.

"Damn!" Rafe jumped back.

Marrok took off after his mate and the wolves who hunted her. His long strides ate up the ground as his enhanced sense of smell allowed him to keep a decent pace and stick to the trail. After about ten minutes, though, he skidded to a halt. The obvious trail went off to his left, but his wolf insisted they go right, a gut-level instinct telling him he'd find his mate in this direction.

He wasted time debating what the facts told him versus what his soul told him was true. If he chose wrong, he'd never get to her in time. His wolf made the decision for him, taking off to the right.

Twenty more minutes of running—the sounds of the woods fading under the steady beat of his feet against the ground and the rush of air in his lungs—and the trail, or whatever pulled him through the woods, went cold.

Marrok stopped and stood in silence. He engaged all the enhanced senses at his disposal to search the trees around him. His wolf whimpered. Had he chosen wrong?

A soft whistle caught his attention. Marrok whipped his head around to look straight up into the eyes of the woman he loved. Tala, in her human form, perched high in the branches of a tall, slender pine tree.

"Thank the gods."

At her answering smile, relief and realization flooded his system in a simultaneous rush. She was safe. He'd found her in time. And he loved her and hadn't told her so. He had no idea when convenience had turned to respect and had become love. All he knew was that losing her would've killed him.

He changed forms before he consciously thought to do so. He needed to hold her in his arms, assure himself she was real. While his body realigned, she must've scrambled down the tree, because when Marrok rose, she slammed into him and coiled herself around his body, and he pulled her even closer, breathing in her sweet scent, grateful as hell he'd found her.

After a long moment just holding her, Marrok pulled back, though he didn't let her go. "Are you okay? Hurt?"

She shook her head, her blond hair falling into her eyes. "Bruises, scrapes from jumping tree to tree. Nothing that won't heal. How'd you find me?" She scrunched her nose.

Without her saying, he knew she was chagrined at being tracked so easily. He brushed the hair back from her face and tucked it behind her ear. "I don't know. My wolf knew you were this way. Did you lay a false path?"

She leaned into his touch. "Yes. Then doubled back in the trees."

Pride joined the layers of relief and love vying for his attention. "You're incredible."

She grimaced. "My own people are trying to kill me. Maybe incredible is a strong term."

"Not all of them."

She frowned her question.

"I've been in touch with Astra. She says only eight or nine wolves appear to be in on this attempted coup. No one else is involved."

Green eyes clouded, like dirty glass. "That doesn't mean much. I'm losing my pack, Marrok."

Because of him. She left that part unsaid, but it floated between them.

"What now?"

Tala grinned, though the deadly glint in her eyes made her smile more evil than humorous, and he frowned.

"Now I'm going to kill them," she said.

He'd been right to be wary. At the same time, he understood. Any wolf who challenged an alpha knew the law. Win the challenge or die, or, if you were lucky, be exiled. But Tala had shown Sandalio mercy, and it bit her in the ass. Now she had something to prove to her people.

Which meant he couldn't help. Again. Already his wolf was growling at the thought of letting her fight on her own.

"Get me back to the crash," she said. "I need my things."

"Is your wolf going to maul me again?"

She grimaced but gave the question due consideration. "I think," she said slowly, "like when we fought Kaios together, she'll be focused on the more immediate threat."

Marrok wasn't as confident. "I'll change first."

Tala chuckled. "Scared of poor little me?"

"Damn straight." He forced his body through the change and, once he was set, she did the same. As soon as she finished and focused on him, a low growl ripped from her, but she took off through the trees rather than attack, so he followed.

While her wolf snarled at him any time he came in her line of sight, she kept going. They made it back to the scene of the crash to find not only Marrok's forces, but many of Tala's. She nodded at her people before moving to the back of the SUV. Shifting with only a small grunt at the end, no doubt more injured than she'd let on, she pulled out her suitcase and immediately stripped off her fancy blouse.

Marrok, who also shifted, stepped between her and the others. Tala was his woman, his mate, and his to appreciate naked. No other man's.

She glanced over her shoulder and rolled her eyes. "This possessive streak is going to be a pain."

"Uh-huh." He grunted without moving.

She snickered before turning back to her suitcase. After dressing in formfitting black pants and a matching tank top and strapping black boots to her feet, she wound the thin chain—the one Marrok knew intimately—around her slim waist. A wicked-looking halter holding a set of small knives went around her shoulders to be hidden under a leather vest. He didn't see what else she stashed on her person, but, knowing Tala, she was loaded down with weapons of various kinds.

"Why didn't you do this earlier?" he asked.

"No time." She turned to face the gathering. "Follow me."

Retracing her original steps, she moved them off the road—where unsuspecting humans might cross their path at any second—and into a small clearing not visible from passersby. "When they come, I deal with them. Alone."

Tala cast a hard stare around those gathered. Every pair

of eyes except his dropped before her gaze, unable to face her head on. They couldn't when she was throwing off alpha vibes the way she was.

"You can't intervene." That glare was aimed his way now.

"I know," he agreed softly.

"I want your word."

That she would take his word told him *some* trust had been built, but hope couldn't penetrate the fear for her life currently gripping his heart with razor-sharp talons. His mate was about to go up against six male wolf shifters on her own.

"You have it." His wolf, however, might not be as controlled.

Chapter Twelve

They didn't have to wait long until the six wolves on her tail found her and Marrok's return markers, and slunk into the clearing, hackles raised, teeth bared, regarding all gathered there with wary hate blazing from glowing eyes. The traitors knew they had no option but to challenge Tala openly, unable to deny being a part of the plot against her. Their scents were all over the car and the woods.

Sandalio she recognized immediately. Hard not to. The remaining five included Dolph, Sandalio's two sons and only grandson, and her cousin Connor, who came as a shock. She never would have guessed family opposed her. The heavy weight of sadness dragged at her heart because now she had to kill him. Kill her own blood.

But he'd made his choice.

Tala stood in the center of the gathering, legs planted wide, hands loose at her sides. The rest of their people, Marrok included, remained at the edge of the clearing where the trees started, giving the area the feel of a boxing ring.

Rather than make the first move, Tala waited in silence.

Someone else was going to have to ding the metaphorical starting bell. In all likelihood, Sandalio and his wolves had discussed their plan before confronting her there. No way could they miss the presence of many of both packs as they traced her path.

Rather than watching their eyes, Tala focused on the torso of the dark gray wolf in the middle—Sandalio. Of course, he was the leader. She studied the movement of his body, staring at a spot mid-chest. She'd learned long ago that eyes might lie, but the body would telegraph what moves were coming.

Taking deep, calming breaths, she readied herself for what she was about to do.

As one, the six wolves lunged for her, deep growls ripping from their throats. In a flash, Tala drew out two knives from her vest. Rather than back up, she rolled toward them and, using her momentum, hurled her weapons as she came up from the roll. Two of the wolves—Sandalio's son and grandson, dropped to the ground with a thud, the blades embedded between their eyes.

Back on her feet, Tala snatched the metal whip from around her waist. With a flick of her wrist, she sliced open Sandalio's face just as his hot breath hit her. He pulled up from his charge, giving her space to crack the whip, wrapping it around Connor's legs. She tugged, setting it to tighten if he struggled. Three down.

Before she could reset, though, a pair of massive arms came around her neck from behind, squeezing the life from her and threatening to crush her bones.

"Watch her, Dolph," Sandalio warned, his voice slithering through her mind. "She always has a blade on her."

Damn straight. As a female wolf shifter, smaller than the males in wolf form by a third or more, her ability with weapons was a strength—one she'd exploit to her dying breath. That ability had made her alpha. Tala stomped her foot, activating a mechanism in her boot which thrust switchblades out of both the toe and the heel.

Using a self-defense maneuver, she dropped into a crouch, leaning forward, which made it harder for Dolph to squeeze her or pick her up. She thrust her hands in front of her, locking her elbows, which loosened his grip slightly, then jammed her right hand straight back behind her with a karate move, right into his balls. To give him credit, Dolph didn't let go fully, but she'd created enough space that now she could swing her leg. She kicked her heel backward, aiming for his shin. The knife point hit bone with a satisfying crunch, and Dolph released her with a howl of rage and agony.

He dropped to the ground, hand over his shin. "Bitch," he spat.

Tala had already slipped her Kubotan from the pouch on her sleeve. Hand gripped around it, she slammed the end of the hard instrument into his temple. Down went Dolph. Dead or unconscious, she didn't give a shit.

Sandalio and his other son hadn't stood still, though. The lighter gray wolf shifter charged as she turned back to them. She couldn't move out of the way fast enough, and his jaws snapped shut around her arm. Tala cried out as shards of pain splintered out from the bite. Her bones broke with a sickening crack. The wolf locked his jaw and shook her like he was trying to shake the stuffing out of a toy. Vaguely she was aware of a thundering growl followed by shouts and yelps.

Marrok must be going crazy. Only he'd promised.

The wolf dropped her to the ground. Tala lay there, head spinning, pain spiking up her arm and consuming her focus, a limp, broken woman. She allowed the tears of frustration and rage to escape her eyes, trailing down her cheeks. Visibly trembling, she held up her damaged arm, as though to ward off the wolf, her limb a mangled mess of blood and bone.

"Don't kill me," she pleaded in a small voice.

The wolf stood over her, his feet on either side of her, waiting for the kill order from his leader.

"So weak. You never were worthy to lead." Sandalio stood at her head now, looming. He gave a nod.

A snarl ripped from his son before he lunged for her neck. Only Tala moved faster. With her one good hand, she whipped one of the steel sticks from a pouch at her ankle and jammed it up through the soft spot under the wolf's jaw, through the soft palate of his mouth and into his brain. Just as she had with his father, only that time she'd spared his life. Not with this one.

She rolled out from under him before he could collapse on top of her and pin her to the ground. Shoving to her feet, she faced Sandalio, who stared at the body of his son as a sickly pallor crept over his face.

"I guess age doesn't always come with wisdom," Tala spat.

"Mercy." The plea echoed through her mind as a whisper.

She held back a grim smile. Sandalio never was a fighter on his own. He'd always relied on numbers and smarts and vicious whispers in dark corners. A glance revealed Marrok, in wolf form, barely held back by six of his own.

"I won't kill you," she said. "I believe my worthiness to lead should no longer be in doubt by the rest of the pack." She glanced around the clearing. Her words weren't a question, but a statement. The emotions reflected back at her told her she'd won her people's respect. Again.

For now, at least.

Relief, almost comic in its intensity, passed over Sandalio's features, his jowls quivering. *"Thank you."*

"I can't say the same for my mate, however." She nodded at the wolves holding Marrok back.

"No!" the traitor shouted.

They moved aside, and the black wolf was on the gray in

one massive leap. He had Sandalio by the neck in an instant. With a vicious snarl, he shook Sandalio until he went limp, then dropped him in a pool of his own blood.

Marrok stood over the body, fur standing on his back, teeth bared, as he growled over the corpse, crazed eyes trained on the others around him.

The general rule of thumb was never to come between a wolf and its kill, but Tala stepped forward. "Hey," she said softly.

The black wolf turned stunning blue eyes her way, glowing with power and rage. He growled again, but more softly now. A hand raised toward him, she moved closer.

"Tala," Astra hissed from the safety of the trees. Tala ignored her sister.

"I need you here. Marrok, do you hear me? I need you to come back to me."

The wolf looked from her to the body on the ground, and back to her. "He's dead. He can't hurt me ever again. You made sure of that."

The wolf quivered, indecision flickering as he held his ground.

"Marrok," she whispered. "Come back to me, mate."

He took one hesitant step forward, then paused, shook his head, and backed up.

Damn. She tried another tack. "I need you inside me, mate." Screw her own pride. She didn't care who was listening. "I need to be claimed."

Blue eyes flared wide, and the wolf gave a soft snort, then moved toward her. Tala held still. Those around them held their collective breath. But he didn't harm her. Instead he rubbed up against her outstretched hand, fur both soft and prickly against her palm, his rumble of satisfaction buzzing against her skin. Then the familiar shimmering surrounded him, and gradually man replaced wolf.

Feverishly, he ran his gaze over her, giving a growl as he caught sight of her maimed arm hanging at a twisted angle at her side. That would hurt like a bitch to straighten but had to be done in order to heal properly. With a strangely choked noise at the back of his throat, Marrok tugged her into his arms, careful not to disturb the injured arm.

"Did you actually just ask to be fucked in front of everyone?"

Of course that's what he'd remember. Her lips tipped up. "I wouldn't put it *quite* like that."

He huffed a laugh but remained serious. "Thanks for giving me the final kill. I don't think I could have come back from the change without my wolf knowing he'd protected his mate first." He gave a shuddering exhale, breath brushing against her cheek.

That he and his wolf cared, warmed her from the inside out. The thought of losing her pack made her sick, but now she had a mate. A true mate, who would never abandon her. Tala stilled in his arms, her mind and heart turning that thought over. She'd never be alone, and that was good.

His protection no longer felt like chains.

Because I love him.

Love... She loved her mate. God, she'd been such a fool. Happiness burst inside her like sunshine burning through early morning haze, the only dark cloud the question of his feelings for her. This was a mating of convenience, arranged for the sake of both their packs.

Still, he was her mate and committed. They could start there. "Let's go home," she whispered.

He huffed a laugh. "Yours or mine?"

"Better start with mine if you don't want to do this again anytime soon." Dominance reestablished, she needed to drive it home.

"Good point."

Chapter Thirteen

Gradually, Tala blinked away the dream that still curled around her like a warm blanket. Marrok's mountains and rum scent surrounded her. She adored waking to that scent, to his warm, hard body against hers every morning. Could she keep him, though?

In the dream, she and Marrok had frolicked in the woods in their wolf forms. He'd nip at her playfully, and her wolf nipped back. She didn't lunge and bare her teeth as had happened every fucking time they tried to be together that way.

For two months.

Ever since she'd had to put five of her pack down for trying to kidnap and kill her—Connor she'd exiled—things had been better. Fantastic even. Marrok was the most attentive mate anyone could ask for—considerate, kind, funny. Okay, a tad possessive and overprotective and still regularly oblivious. He couldn't help himself. But more in the ways of a clueless mate these days. Tala smiled thinking about how he'd practically snapped Castor's head off when the demigod had hugged her at his and Leia's wedding.

At the same time, Marrok's respect for her as alpha was unwavering. She was included in every decision. He deferred to her frequently, in fact. After six months of living part time in each pack, they'd finally agreed on a new location where they would combine packs permanently. Construction started next week.

The only fly in her ointment was her wolf. Mates played together as wolves, ran together, hunted together, fought together. Okay, her animal *would* fight side by side with Marrok, but that had happened on only a handful of occasions.

Her wolf snorted, as disturbed by the dream as she, and laid her head on her paws. A wave of frustration skittered through Tala, coming from her wolf.

Why? If you're frustrated that's not us, then why? You're the one holding back.

Her wolf snorted again.

Tala's cell rang, interrupting the daily argument with her wilder half.

With a sigh she checked the number and frowned. Brimstone. She clicked the button to answer. "Delilah?"

"I've given you six months to figure it out." Her friend never wasted time with pleasantries.

"Figure what out?" Tala glanced at Marrok and found him watching her with those bright blue eyes. He lifted his eyebrows in curiosity. She shrugged.

A *tsk* came down the line. "Your wolf is trying to tell you something, love."

No shit.

"What exactly? Because I can't figure her out?"

"You're an alpha."

Still not following. "So?"

"So is she."

"Okay?"

Another *tsk*. "*Claim* your mate."

She might as well have added "dumbass" at the end of that, because Tala had been dense on this topic.

The lightbulb finally clicked on. How had she missed it? The night of their mating, Marrok had given her a claiming bite. Her wolf growled every time he licked those silvery scars, which would never fade, unlike other injuries. Until that moment, her wolf had been even more eager for her mate than Tala had. Then she'd gone cold.

"Gotta go." Tala hung up and dropped the phone on the floor.

She jumped out of the bed. Ignoring her naked state, she threw a pair of jeans folded neatly in a chair at Marrok. "Get dressed."

She hustled into her own jeans and T-shirt and slapped on a pair of running shoes.

"What's the rush?" Amusement rife in his voice, Marrok hitched a half smile her direction, one that made her heart beat faster, and she didn't bother to control it.

He laughed, and she knew he heard the change in rhythm. Marrok always seemed to gain pleasure from making her lose her cool.

"Come on." She tugged him until they were outside, then she ran into the woods, knowing he'd follow.

"Where are we going?"

"My favorite spot."

The location in question was an idyllic glen beside a babbling stream. The glen was situated next to a natural pool, though the water was often too chilly to swim in. Tala loved the spot for its quiet perfection. She could go there and let go of the pressures of her life. Even if for a short time.

"Fine by me." Satisfaction replaced his amusement. She didn't have to turn around to know his smile had turned into glittering desire. The emotion curled around her through their link. No wonder. She'd shared her spot with Marrok a few times over the last months. Now the place held intimate memories.

"And are you going to have your wicked way with me there?" he asked, fingers laced with hers.

"I'm going to claim you as my mate." Not much farther now.

Marrok went quiet on her, but she didn't dare face him until they reached their destination.

The glen welcomed them with warm breezes rattling through the aspen grove close by, the leaves a glorious golden yellow. Tala turned, ready to explain things, only to run into a wall of muscle. Marrok claimed her lips in a kiss meant to conquer. He picked her up by the ass and she wrapped her legs around him, reveling in the hard evidence of his desire thrust against her.

In a swift move only a supernatural could make, he laid them on the ground. With a growl he pulled back. "If you think you're going to claim me and show me how dominant you are…"

Disappointment hitched in her throat. Would he deny her this? Deny them?

Suddenly he rolled so she was on top, straddling him. He tucked his hands behind his head and grinned. "I'm all yours."

Tala laughed, then quickly sobered, as eager to claim her mate as her wolf, who was panting for it. Just to teach him a small lesson, she raked her nails down his chest, shredding his T-shirt and leaving long, red welts on the skin beneath.

His smile disappeared, skin tightening over his cheekbones. This time, his heart joined hers in a rapid tattoo of beats.

With concise movements she stripped them both of their clothing. No need for more foreplay; he was as ready as she.

With a moan of pleasure, she sank down on his shaft, filled with him, stretched by him in the most delicious way. She dug her nails into his pecs, adding to the marks she'd left on him already, and slowly started to move her hips, setting a rhythm meant to tease, meant to build their desire.

"Woman, you must be trying to kill me." But he didn't stop her or force her faster.

Hands at her hips, gripping hard, he watched with fascination in his eyes that only drove her own desire.

Across their mating link he fed her heat, and need, and an awe that she was his, something she reflected back at him. No need for pheromones.

Sending him a smile a siren would envy, Tala leaned forward, letting the tips of her breasts brush his chest, her nipples tightening at the contact with his warm flesh. She ran her hands up his arms and tangled their fingers together as she set a faster pace. Climax would come fast for both of them today. Already he thickened inside her.

Freeing her wolf slightly, her canines dropped in her mouth. With nibbling kisses, she moved across his jaw to the spot where his neck curved into his shoulder and lightly scraped at the skin there with her teeth, pulling a deep groan from him.

As her orgasm built, tingling and pooling deep inside her, she licked at the spot, marking it as hers.

Marrok bucked beneath her, and a starburst of pleasure exploded inside them both. In that instant, she sank her teeth into his flesh, claiming her mate for all time. Her wolf howled as something snapped into place inside her head.

Marrok.

She could feel him inside her, so much stronger than before—his emotions, his state of being. As though she'd been muting him and had turned up the volume.

Her mate was…happy. Elated.

Her mate...*loved her.*

The sensation of his orgasm slammed into her through the connection, tipping her into another one, the waves of pleasure battering against her, and all she could do was hold on for the ride until they both slowed.

Breathing hard, she pulled her teeth back and curled over him, catching her breath.

"You love me?" she whispered, awe stripping her of her usual coolness. In six months, neither had said the words. She'd held back, waiting for their relationship to develop, giving him time to feel...something for her. She'd hoped and wondered.

Marrok threaded his fingers through her hair and lifted so that he could place a sweet kiss against her lips. "I thought that was obvious," he murmured.

Tala shook her head, overwhelmed by emotions only this man could elicit from her. "I love you, too."

Another grin. "I know."

A silence fell over the glen, deafening in the absence of sound.

Everything around them stilled unnaturally. Not a breeze, not a bird call, not a whisper of sound. With twin frowns, Tala and Marrok both levered up, his arm wrapped around her, to find every creature of the nearby forest surrounding them— birds, chipmunks, deer, elk, even a wolf and a bear. To Tala it seemed as though every plant, every drop of water, even the sun was focused solely on them.

As one, the animals bowed their heads. Even the trees seemed to dip in deference to them. Then, as one, the creatures turned and disappeared into the mountainside beyond. Sound returned to the glen and the breeze whispered through the trees once again.

"A sign from the gods," Tala whispered. For them? "What does it mean?"

She turned to Marrok, whose eyes blazed blue. A smile tugged at his lips. "It means, mate, our union was always fated. We no longer have that lie hanging over us. Everything else...we'll figure out as we go."

With a sigh she sank into a sweet kiss she never wanted to end.

Her wolf, however, was eager to accept her mate at last. Tala pulled back with a grin. "Run with me."

This time she didn't worry as she shifted, as happy to finally let their wolves run together as her wolf was. Within minutes they stood together, white and black wolves. Tala gave her mate a playful nip before she took off into the forest.

With a joyful yelp, he followed.

Epilogue

Delilah smiled at her phone, knowing Tala and Marrok would be all right now. Sometimes a person couldn't see what was under their nose. It took a neutral—well, mostly neutral—third party to see the truth more clearly.

That and some pretty wicked skills when it came to seeing the future.

She'd known when she'd suggested the arranged mating that all roads would eventually lead to this point. Of course, as stubborn as Tala and Marrok were, they'd taken the longer path to get here. But their bond was strong, and their leadership would guarantee that Banes and Canis clans, eventually, would not only find peace, but also harmony.

A soft knock at her door pulled her out of her thoughts. "Come in," she called.

Her assistant, Naiobe, entered with Rowan MacAuliffe. The redheaded witch in her custody was still a problem. After being forced to use her powers against the nymphs at Tala and Marrok's mating, Rowan was in deep trouble. The Covens Syndicate that governed all magic users had set one of their best hunters on Rowan's trail, and Delilah couldn't keep her hidden much longer.

Blood was in the water, and the sharks were circling.

Despite all that, Rowan had refused to share much of herself or how she'd become involved in the attack. Not only that, but the Syndicate seemed to have no record of her, which was, in and of itself, fascinating.

Rowan needed help, even if she refused to accept it.

Delilah waited until the other woman took the chair across the desk from her—feet crossed at the ankles, hands in her lap, making herself small with her shoulders hunched forward and gaze trained on the ground.

Leaning forward, Delilah waited until Rowan finally lifted her gaze and met her eyes. "So you still don't trust me?"

Rowan glanced around the room, wary as a cornered mountain lion, but nodded. "Don't take it personally. I don't trust anyone."

You're not the only one. Delilah allowed herself a small smile as she brought up the case file that had given her an idea of what to do next with Rowan. "Be that as it may, I've managed to get to the truth of your situation."

Stunning gray eyes focused on her with narrowed distrust. "And?"

"And I can help you. If you'd like."

The plan she had in mind was damn risky, especially for Rowan. But she suspected the witch was no stranger to risk. Or deceit.

Will she agree to my proposal? For once, the future wasn't as certain as Delilah liked.

Acknowledgments

No matter what is going on in my life, I get to live out my dream surrounded and supported by the people I love—a blessing that I thank God for every single day. Writing and publishing a book doesn't happen without the support and help from a host of incredible people.

To my readers (especially my Awesome Nerds Facebook fan group!)... Thanks for going on this ride with me. Sharing my worlds with you is a huge part of the fun. Tala and Marrok were a blast to write, with both of them needing to make the relationship work, but hard to do when you're both an alpha. And phew, the heat! I hope you loved these two wolf shifters as much as I loved writing them. If you have a free sec, please think about leaving a review. Also, I love to connect with my readers, so I hope you'll drop a line and say "Howdy" on any of my social media!

To my editor, Heather Howland...This is book number ten or eleven together, and I loved working with you on every single one. Thanks for being the best and making my writing sparkle!

To my Entangled family...best team in the business! Love you all!

To my agent, Evan Marshall...my voice of reason and direction. You're the best!

To my author sisters and friends...you are the people I feel most *me* with, and you inspire me every single day.

To my support team of beta readers, critique partners, writing buddies, reviewers, RWA chapters (even with the blowup), friends, and family (you know who you are)...thank you, thank you, thank you.

Finally, to my own partner in life and our awesome kids...I don't know how it's possible, but I love you more every day.

About the Author

Award-winning paranormal romance author Abigail Owen grew up consuming books and exploring the world through her writing. She loves to write witty, feisty heroines, sexy heroes who deserve them, and a cast of lovable characters to surround them (and maybe get their own stories). She currently resides in Austin, Texas, with her own personal hero, her husband, and their two children, who are growing up way too fast.

Discover more Amara titles...

FURY UNLEASHED
a *Forgotten Brotherhood* novel by N.J. Walters

Maccus Fury, a fallen angel, is trying hard to keep his sanity. Seems being an assassin might be catching up with him. Now, Heaven, or Hell, has sent a beautiful assassin to kill him. Lovely. She's smart and snarky—but she has no idea what she's walked into. And he's more than peeved that they only sent one person. They're going to need an army if they want him dead.

MALFUNCTION
a *Dark Desires Origin* novel by Nina Croft

It's been five hundred years since we fled a dying Earth. Twenty-four ships, each carrying ten thousand humans—Chosen Ones—sleeping peacefully...until people start dying in cryo. Malfunction or murder? Sergeant Logan Farrell is determined to find the truth. Katia Mendoza, hot-shot homicide detective, has been woken from cryo to assist his investigation, and Logan finds himself falling for her. But he doesn't know Katia's secret... It's not only humans who fled the dying Earth.

SHIFTER PLANET: THE RETURN
a novel by D.B. Reynolds

Scientist Rachel Fortier thinks she'd on the tiny planet of Harp to study the planet's wild cats. But her shipmates have a darker purpose. And when they capture a gorgeous golden panther, she discovers they intend to keep it--for experimentation! Rachel has to free him. But when she does, she learns two things... One, her cat is a shifter. And two, he's the most beautiful man she's ever met.

Made in United States
Troutdale, OR
06/17/2024

20622424R00075